COSPLAY
and
Confrontation

SARAH ZANE

Cosplay and Confrontation
Copyright © 2023 by Sarah Cuenca
Published by The Library of Sarah Zane

All rights reserved, including the right to reproduce this book in any form whatsoever. This is a work of fiction. Names, characters, places, and incidents either are the product of the author's imagination or are used fictitiously. Any resemblance to actual persons, living or dead, businesses, companies, events, or locales is entirely coincidental.

Ebook ISBN: 979-8-9861080-4-9
Paperback ISBN: 979-8-9861080-6-3

Cover Design: MiblArt
Editing and Formatting: Genevieve A. Scholl

www.libraryofsarahzane.com

To the girl with the ocean eyes for making me learn to love the caramel whiskey in mine.

And to all the queers out there still looking for their fairytale love or their found family…
Keep looking, they're out there and will find you sooner or later.

"Could there be finer symptoms? Is not general incivility the very essence of love?"

Pride and Prejudice by Jane Austen

Chapter One

Gwen

When I saw the email from Kodie, my heart dropped. I knew it was coming. The date was getting closer and closer, and I would have to face her sooner or later. She was kind enough that I knew she would be understanding about me dropping out of the convention, but it was obvious I was letting her down. I hated that I had to do it, but there was no way I could go home right now, no way I could face Portland yet, no way I could face *her*. Lanie hated my guts, so much so that she changed her social names to spite me. She went by Morgana now. She used to go by Ash, but she would always be Lanie to me.

I missed her deeply, but she had made it abundantly clear that I was dead to her, more dead than my relationship with Arty. She hated me for breaking up with him, but I had to. I couldn't live a lie and I couldn't string him along. She didn't understand, but how could she when I never told her the whole truth?

I was planning to, but she never gave me the chance. She was too angry that night, and I hadn't seen her since.

I felt Ollie lean into me, a strand of his shaggy purple hair brushing my cheek as he read the email over my shoulder. Kodie was just checking in. She hadn't heard from me in a while and wanted to know what changes to make to her advertisements. It was a polite way of saying, 'Hey. I heard about your breakup. Are you chickening out on me, or are you going to come back to the city for the first time in months?' I was most definitely chickening out. I had to.

I couldn't do Books, Gowns, and Crowns on my own when it was supposed to be mine and Lanie's weekend together. Then again, Kodie picked me. She had picked and trusted me to help her boost attendance for the event. Not that she needed it with some of the big authors she had on the roster, but I had agreed to help and I knew some of my followers were going specifically to see me.

Books, Gowns, and Crowns was a multi-day book lover's paradise packed with book sales, author signings, and meet and greets with influencers, and that wasn't even the best part. They also threw a fantasy ball, complete with ball gowns and crowns, the works. There was even a cosplay contest that I had been really excited about entering with Lanie. We would have dominated.

We were supposed to go as Cassandra and Ivy, the ultimate enemies-to-lovers pair. I had been surprised when Lanie agreed to it. I thought she might think it was an odd choice to go as a sapphic enemies-to-lovers pair, but she hadn't questioned it. She was psyched since Cassandra was her favorite, which was perfect because with my pale complexion, red hair, and freckles, I looked a lot like Ivy.

It was supposed to be a great weekend, just the two of us. It had sounded too good to be true, but now it had turned into a curse. Arty wasn't going to be there, so going was out of the question. If he had been going, maybe I could have gone. He would have been able to get her to communicate with me.

He could have mediated for us, but I couldn't go without him. I couldn't face her on my own.

Not going meant disappointing Kodie and any of my followers that had gotten tickets to see me there, but going meant facing Lanie, seeing the hatred in her eyes as she looked at me. I couldn't do it. I didn't think I could survive it. I would rather disappoint thousands than have to face her.

I sighed. "So I have to tell her."

Ollie nodded. "You do. I know they're sold out, but I'm sure she'll make an exception for Gwen Pendragon, the Queen of Cosplay."

"Huh?"

Ollie and I were always on the same page, but right now I didn't have a clue what he was talking about. Why would I need her to make an exception for me?

"You're going to need an extra ticket for your best friend, bodyguard, boyfriend extraordinaire. Kodie's lucky I'm awesome enough to be all three, otherwise you'd be needing three more tickets." He grinned, but I didn't smile back. I was too shocked. I couldn't go. He had to know that.

"I'm not going," I clarified.

He rolled his eyes. "And you call me dramatic. Of course you're going."

"I can't. You didn't see how it was with her. I can't."

"I didn't have to see it to know you can't let her keep pushing you around. I won't let you. I mean, geez, her name's still up on their website and everything. Doesn't that bother you? She's only up there because you had her put up there."

Of course it bothered me, but not in the way he thought. Every time I saw our pictures together, it bothered me; every time I saw her, I had to fight my fingers from itching to reach for my phone. I kept hoping that missing her would get easier, but it didn't.

I had thought about letting Kodie know what happened, about having Lanie removed as my co-cosplayer. I could if I wanted to. Lanie was up there because she was my plus one. As an influencer at the event, I was allowed to bring one person. It would've been a hard choice, but Arty was going to be out of town, and Lanie agreed to be the other half to my cosplay. I could have asked any of the guys besides Arty, but having Lanie come felt natural. I wanted her there, and so Kodie added her up there with me. The thought of her picture coming off the website was too much for me. The thought of not getting to see her dark eyes staring out at me, of not getting to her light brown skin around her eyes wrinkle as she smirked out at the camera, was too much for me. It would kill me to see anyone else's picture next to mine there. At least on the website we were still together.

I couldn't say any of that out loud, not even to Ollie. It was too pathetic. I was pathetic. I couldn't face her.

"I can't," was all I said.

"You have to. You let her push you around and intimidate you for too long. I mean, geez, you ran to San Fran to hide from her. She ran you out of your own city. You can't let her keep feeling like she won."

He didn't get it, but again, that was my fault. He didn't know the whole truth about the breakup. Only Arty and I did. I respected and loved Arty too much to not give him the whole truth; he deserved to know.

A tiny part of me had worried Arty would tell people, but I shouldn't have worried because he never did. That was Arty for you, chivalrous and kind at all times. It didn't matter to him that his political career was affected. He never sold me out. He never told the truth, never fed me to the wolves, and even if

I spent the rest of my life trying to pay him back for that kindness, it would never be enough.

It would never be enough, because he never asked for anything in return. He was kind for the sake of being kind and genuinely wanted to make the world a better place. He was impossible to be mad at and was even harder to break up with. Even while I was breaking up with him, he was asking about my feelings and comforting me. It was clear to everyone I never deserved him, and I was repaying his kindness by continuing to hide, continuing to lie. I hated that, but I didn't know if I was strong enough to face the consequences yet.

At least, not alone. Maybe, with Ollie, I could.

"You'd really come with me?"

Without hesitation, he replied, "You couldn't stop me if you tried."

"You know what people will think, though."

"And?"

"And what if they're mean to you?"

He locked at me a moment, considering, before grinning. "With this face? They don't stand a chance."

I laughed at that. He was all charm and bravado, but I knew it was for my sake. It couldn't have been easy; what I was asking him to do. Being my boyfriend wasn't an easy task in general, but it definitely wasn't an easy one for this public of an appearance.

"Are you sure you're ready for that?"

He grinned. "Ready? Please, they aren't ready for me."

I laughed again. One thing was for sure, Portland wasn't going to know what hit them when he got to town.

Chapter Two

Lanie

 Every single day. Every damn day I checked that stupid website waiting to see the only thing that would let me breathe. Waiting to not have to see her calculating smile looking back at me. Waiting for the inevitable angry fans and fallout from her dropping out. Everyone who hadn't already turned on her would then. Once they knew how truly selfish she was, they would all see things my way. Be on my side. Well, Arty's side really.

 How anyone still supported her after she broke his heart, never mind how four-hundred-fifty-thousand someones still supported her, I would never understand.

I kept waiting for her to drop out, the anticipation building with each day. The longer she waited, the better for me and the worse for her.

She and I had planned this together every step of the way, down to our cosplays. I had been shocked when she suggested Cassandra and Ivy. People would jump so far to conclusions, but she insisted, and I agreed. After all, we were dead ringers for the two of them. Now, Arty had a broken heart, she had a new boyfriend, and I was stuck with this feeling of betrayal and one half of a couple's cosplay.

I'd be damned if I let her change any facet of my plans, though. I tried in vain to find a new Ivy. I even resorted to dating websites that I used to shudder at the thought of, but no one worked out.

At least I had my friends going. They tried to convince me to join their A Ripple of Power and Promise cosplay, but I already had the Cassandra outfits ready. And if I was being honest, I wanted the satisfaction of her seeing the photos online and knowing I didn't shy away from our plans.

I needed her to know she didn't win, and I couldn't think of a better way.

She only had a couple of weeks left, and yet her stupid face was still on their website, taunting me. She was cutting this real close. I couldn't believe how close, but it would be any day now. I knew without a doubt she wouldn't be coming. Just like she had let me down, she would let her fans down. She wouldn't come back. Not to Portland. She wouldn't dare. Portland was my city. Well, Portland was our city. Our Camelot, so to speak.

Arty would be laughing if he knew I thought of it that way. Yes, he cosplayed as King Arthur, but it was just that, cosplay. He didn't know the stories like I did. With his light skin and blonde hair, he looked the part, but it was more than that. For me, King Arthur was an idealistic, honorable man, one worth fighting for and worth looking up to. Arty hit all those marks for me. He was the very definition of chivalrous, without an ounce of pretension. Arty pushed for equality for everyone. A regular social justice warrior in the most idealistic sense of the word. At some point, I started looking up to him, and I never stopped.

I tasked myself with protecting him from the outside world. I wouldn't let anyone or anything hurt him. He was a light in the darkness, hope for a hopeless world, and I would make sure no one even so much as dimmed that in him.

I had vowed to protect him. Well, internally vowed. I'm fairly certain if I had made that vow to him, he would have laughed, but I was serious, and I had succeeded, until her.

She sauntered her way into the picture, fiery red hair and a personality to match, and those ocean blue eyes you could drown in. She fit right into our little duo, like a missing puzzle piece. If Arty was goodness incarnate, she was sunshine. Around her, everything was brighter.

Them getting together was the most natural thing in the world. Knowing the two of them, it made perfect sense. They were both always so optimistic and happy. At least, she always seemed so happy. It wasn't until she called Arty and me crying one night that we realized how deeply she buried her own hurt. We knew she had been going through a hard breakup, but didn't know how hard until that night.

She had told us she had something to do that night, and Arty hadn't asked. She had been spending almost every minute with us, so it was unusual, but since he didn't ask, I didn't either.

We didn't find out until much later that what she was doing was going back to her ex's place to get her stuff back. She hadn't told us he was holding some of her treasured possessions hostage. Of course she hadn't. We wouldn't have let him.

She told us later that she was trying to be brave and handle things herself. It wasn't brave; it was foolish.

Arty and I were halfway across the city when she called crying. The half-hour drive took ten minutes. I didn't touch the brakes. She was in the stacks of Powell's, on the second floor, huddled in a deep corner with Pride and Prejudice, dried tears still obvious on her face.

I remember the relief and annoyance at seeing her crying over a book. I loved Gwen, we both did, and we would've gone regardless, but if I had known it was over a book, I would've broken less traffic laws to get there.

I was about to say so when my eyes landed on her wrist. Her sweatshirt sleeves had fallen a little, enough to expose a dark ring around her wrist. I saw red. She looked at me and tried to smile, but her face fell the moment she tracked my gaze. She looked in horror at her arm, rolling her sleeve up quickly, but it was too late.

Arty rushed to her and pulled her into him, and I could hear her tears, hear the pain in her sobs, the panic. What I would've given for her to have been upset over Pride and Prejudice.

She didn't say anything for a long time, and he just held her. I shuffled on my feet, feeling awkward and out of place for the first time since she joined our trio.

After her breathing slowed, Arty looked over at me and nodded. I managed a few clipped words. "Who and where?"

She pulled away from Arty quickly, looking at me in horror. She didn't need more; she understood from the look in my eye. "I don't want either of you getting hurt."

"Trust me, it won't be us getting hurt."

Her tears started again, and I fell to my knees in front of her, on the ground with her and Arty. "Tell me what to do. Tell me how to help," I whispered.

"I just need somewhere to stay. This was the only place I felt safe right now. I needed to escape." She looked around, taking in me and Arty and the stacks themselves. She took a deep breath and said with resolve, "I think I need a more permanent escape, though." She looked at Arty and blurted out, "I know it's asking a lot, and you can definitely say no, and I'm so sorry I have to ask, but I really don't have anyone to turn to. No one would believe me. I just need to get out, and I need a place to stay for a little while, only until I can get back on my own two feet. I guess what I'm asking is..."

She looked back and forth between me and him. I knew exactly what she was asking and my answer, but she wasn't asking me. She had asked Arty.

He waited a few more moments for her to finish her thought, but she didn't say anything. I urged him with my eyes to say something. He was far more patient than I was. I wouldn't have waited, but he wanted to give her time to think, but she wouldn't even look up from the floor to meet his eye.

He looked at me, questioning. I nodded. How he thought for even a moment I might say no was beyond me.

He turned his attention back to Gwen, took her head in his hands, and turned her chin upward to look at him. "Gwen, you don't even have to ask. You can stay with us as long as you'd like."

Her eyes brightened, and tears began anew. "Really?" she asked, looking from him to me. I nodded. It wasn't even a question. There wasn't anything I wouldn't do for her.

"Of course. For as long as you like. We could grow old together if you wanted," Arty said.

I bit back my laugh when I saw her blush. His honesty took some getting used to. A moment later, he blushed, and added, "I didn't mean it like that. Just that you have a place with us for as long as you want it. I would never ask you to leave, not until you say you want to."

She came home with us that night, and we welcomed her light in our lives. She was the reason Sam, Eli, and Ben started coming over more. She instituted mandatory "family" dinners and mandatory group game nights. Arty and Sam loved that, and as much as Eli, Ben, and I grumbled about it, we all secretly did, too. She brought a new life to us all. Her, Arty, and I were inseparable, and I got used to it. I found myself hoping she would stick around forever, and I thought she would, until the night she fled. The night she broke Arty's heart. The night I caught her with *him*.

I should have known. I had read all the legends, and every damned one, every reiteration of the story, said that Gwen would be bad news for Arty. Every damned story, Gwen betrayed Arthur. It was a bad omen, but I let my guard down. She got under my skin, and I let her in. I trusted her, and the way he looked at her warmed something inside of me. I fell for her, too, in a way. She was sunshine; it was hard not to feel warmed by her. But that's the problem with sunshine; when it exits your life, all you're left with is darkness.

She took every ounce of light from us when she left. She made herself the center of our universe and then broke his heart and abandoned us, and for what? For *him*. What the hell did he have that Arty didn't? That I didn't? What the hell did she see in him?

Then it hit me. She had been using Arty and me. She had been using us for a place to stay and probably using him to boost her views online.

Everyone had been calling them a power couple. I wondered what they would think if they knew how she had betrayed him, ripped out his heart and stomped on it for that insignificant man. She must have been cheating for a while, too. You don't up and run away with a guy you just started seeing. That was the part that hurt the most. She ran away to him.

I wanted to make a video that night. I didn't want there to be anywhere she could run or hide from what she did to him, to us, but Arty stopped me. He was too good for her, too good for anyone, really. Even heartbroken and alone, he was protecting her.

I wondered what people would say if they knew Camelot was up in flames. Gwen had run off with Lancelot, leaving Arthur and me alone in the dark.

The darkness devoured us both for a while, but eventually we were able to pick up the pieces and move past it.

I actually had managed to go a couple of weeks without thinking about her, until Books, Gowns, and Crowns was announced and I had to look at her picture up there next to mine.

There wasn't anything crueler, but we were only a few days away now, and she would back out. She had to.

Chapter Three

"She's still there!" I groaned, throwing my phone on my bed, only to pick it up a moment later.

Through the screen, I saw Arty was hiding a smile. Damn him. Nothing about this was funny. "How can you be smiling?! This isn't anywhere near funny. She only has a week left. She can't mean to actually come, right?"

"I know. What a monster, right? Wanting to come to an event she's a big part of? In her own hometown? The humanity! The audacity!"

If it were anyone else, I would've hung up, but this was Arty. I took a breath. "You make me sound like I'm being crazy."

"Wellll......" was all he said. He knew better than to agree, but then again, it was Arty. He was the only one who didn't tiptoe around me when it came to her.

"Don't go there." I ran my free hand over the shaved side of my head, frustrated.

"She has every right to be there, though."

I started pacing, unable to stay still in my aggravation.

"No, she doesn't! Not after what she did to you! What she put you through. She has no right to be back in our city."

I couldn't believe it when he broke into a laugh. "Come on. Even you can't own a whole city."

"I don't. We do."

He laughed harder, before catching his breath and putting his hands up in mock surrender. "Don't drag me into this, Lanie. I don't want any part of your vendettas and vengeance."

He knew I hated being called Lanie. Hated any sort of reminder of her, no matter how small. "Don't call me that! No one can call me that anymore. It's Lane to you, Morgana to everyone else. Besides, this isn't my vengeance to claim. It's yours."

He looked at me for a long moment before shaking his head. "I'll tell you until I'm blue in the face. I don't want vengeance. I'm not angry."

"That makes it worse! You're too good for her. You always were. But even now, when she's betrayed you like she did, you still defend her."

"You're being too harsh on her and too kind to me. Gwen and I-" I glared at him through the screen. He held up his hands in surrender. "Okay, okay. She-who-must-not-be-named and I worked out our issues. I wish her nothing but the best and wish you would leave her alone."

"You can't really mean that," I said, even though I could read the sickening sincerity on his face. He was too good for this world, and definitely too good for her. "Why? Why do you always defend her? Especially when she cheated on you?!"

"Lane," he said with a quiet calm. "That's enough." I was appalled. He never spoke to me like that. It shocked me enough that I listened. "There are things that happened between Gwen and I, things I promised I wouldn't tell a soul."

I started to protest, but he cut me off. "To me, you don't count as a person. You're an extension of me."

"Your better half, right?" I joked.

He grinned. "You know it." Like always, he wasn't joking.

Arty was a special kind of person. He only saw the best in others. He was the optimist to my realist. He only saw the best in me, despite me continually giving him reasons to think worse of me. It was a big part of the reason our friendship worked so well. We were bonded for life, always had been, always would be. Usually, I found his views charming, but not when it came to her. His inability to see anything negative in people blinded him and made him susceptible to be taken advantage of by the worst people. She cheated on him and stomped on his heart. He bore it gracefully and kindly like he did everything, but I knew he was hurting, and hurting him was a criminal offense in my book. He wouldn't stand up for himself, so I had to be his avenging angel.

"But I made a promise, and I won't break it. I wouldn't break my word, especially on this, for the world. I need you to trust me. She's doing the best she can. She doesn't deserve this."

He was feeding me the same lines he kept pushing to his followers that were harassing her. Not the promise part, that was new, but the rest was the same old spiel. I should've expected it by now.

"I know, I know. You're too nice for your own good, but she deserves everything she's gotten. She felt so guilty that she ran away. She couldn't face me or the rest of this city, couldn't be around you, so she ran off to her plaything."

He raised an eyebrow at me. "Her plaything?"

"*Lancelot.*" I sneered.

He broke into howling, knee slapping, gut busting laughter. "That's rich. You don't actually believe in all that, do you?"

"I didn't, but you can't deny the evidence."

He looked at me incredulously. "You can't mean to say I'm some resurrected long-dead King?"

"I wouldn't go that far. Don't be getting a bigger ego on me," I joked.

He put his hand to his heart with a mock surprised gasp. "I would never."

Had he been here, I would have shoved him. Had he been here, things would be different. I wouldn't be preparing for battle on my own. Well, maybe I still would be. This was his battle, but it was one he refused to fight. Maybe it was better he was out of town.

"Honestly, please, for me, go easy on her. After all, it's not her fault she's possessed by some long-dead Queen." I started to protest, but he continued, "You can't have it both ways. Either she's a flawed person doing her best, or she's the reincarnation of a long-dead Queen and didn't have a choice in the matter. Either way, if she does come home, please leave her alone."

"If she comes back alone, I'll go easy on her, but if she brings *him*, all bets are off."

I heard his mother calling him in the background. "I have to go, but please, if she does come back, don't scare her off."

There was a pain in his eyes that made me see red. He wanted her back in our city. He didn't want me to scare her off because he wanted her back here. He might even want *her* back. That wouldn't happen. Not on my watch. If she did come back, I would make sure she didn't feel welcome. I would make sure she knew just what I thought of her and make her pay for the pain in his eyes.

Chapter Four

Gwen

The moment I saw the White Stag, I knew I was home. I was finally home, and this was a terrible plan. Nothing had changed, not really. The problems I was running from were still here. The person I was running from was still here.

If anything had changed, it was me. I could only hope I had changed enough to brave the storm that I knew was coming.

But at least I wasn't alone this time. I breathed a sigh of relief as I felt his fingers interlace with mine. Ollie was here, my own personal protector, bodyguard, best friend, boyfriend extraordinaire. If I wasn't strong enough, I would have to lean on him until I could stand on my own.

It was why he came. He knew, even before I did, how much I would need him this weekend.

This weekend that was supposed to be a fun, happy get together with friends had taken a turn.

Yes, that was all my fault, but I still hoped the weekend was salvageable. It wouldn't be the weekend I imagined. It was only me and now Ollie, but I would still have fun. I had a couple of killer cosplays lined up and some fans to meet. It wouldn't be all bad. As long as I managed to avoid her.

I had tried to back out a couple of times, but couldn't work up the courage, knowing how many people I would be disappointing. A few fans had reached out, telling me they only bought tickets because they knew I was coming.

I couldn't let them down or disappoint anyone like that. I could handle this. I had to. I wouldn't let the ghosts of my past continue to scare me from home. This was my home, too, and it was time to take my life and city back. I was done being haunted, done running.

Arty and I had long ago made peace with everything. We were still friendly, unlike me and Lanie. I wished things could go back to normal with her, but I was beyond hoping I could salvage things. Her opinion of me was too clear. I knew she hated me with every fiber of her being, and I understood. I wished I didn't. On darker days, I even wished I could hate her, but I couldn't.

I had hurt her, badly. Not on purpose. I would have never hurt her on purpose, but she still had every right to hate me.

I should have stayed and tried to fix things. I should've tried to make her understand, but I was a coward. I didn't try. I ran.

Now I was back to face the music, and I knew I wasn't ready, but I was done running.

Chapter Five

So far, so good. I had been back for a whole twelve hours and nothing bad had happened yet. I kept looking over my shoulder, watching, waiting. For what, I really didn't know. It had been months. Maybe she was over it by now.

Maybe, or maybe seeing me again would bring back all her negative feelings.

Maybe I was right to stay away, but I was already here, and I doubted I could avoid her for the rest of my life anyway, especially since I planned to move back.

That was my other goal for this weekend. I was out here looking at apartments, and desperately trying to convince Ollie that moving up here with me would be a good decision.

I could afford it on my own, but the thought of being back in Portland all by myself was too much for me to really consider. Lucky for me, Ollie seemed like he would be easy to convince.

 We had just finished looking at apartments, and his eyes had lit up at the last one. Not surprising, since it was beautiful. It was a modern design with an open concept and high ceilings, but it somehow still felt inviting. Spacious enough that it didn't feel like the walls were closing in on you, spacious enough you felt separated from your neighbors, but not too spacious to not feel cozy.

 It had two bathrooms, one of which had a clawfoot tub next to a floor-to-ceiling window, letting you look out at the city. The tub was separated from the rest of the bathroom by a dividing wall, making it feel private, like its own space.

 The apartment even had a balcony off the living room. I was already picturing the fairy lights I would string up there and the late-night talks Ollie and I could have out there once we put out some lounge chairs. Not that we couldn't talk anywhere, but there was something magical about sitting high above the city under the stars.

 It made you feel anonymous, like you could say anything, powerful, like you could be anyone, do anything. It put life into perspective, showing you how truly small your problems were in the grand scheme of things. Arty, Lanie, and I used to make a game out of making up stories for the ant-sized people passing by. That's one thing I loved so much about cities, and about Portland specifically. There was never a shortage of interesting people.

I missed that. I missed those nights together with them. Missed how carefree they felt, how the world was at our feet and full of possibility. Missed how full my heart felt at being with them both, laughing about nothing and everything. There wasn't anything too private or too weird to share with them. We were so solid nothing could break us. There were no secrets between us... until suddenly there was. A secret so big that it threatened to tear us apart if it came to life. A secret that I tried to bury. A secret that never saw the light of day but tore us apart, anyway. A secret that turned Lanie, my best friend, into Morgana, the woman I had been running from ever since. The woman I almost cancelled my appearance at Books, Gowns, and Crowns to avoid. It felt like the city wasn't big enough for the both of us. Things never used to be like that, but the best I could hope for now was to manage to avoid her the whole weekend and then I could deal with the rest after.

Maybe I was crazy for coming back, crazier still for wanting to move back here permanently. Maybe, but something about the city called me back. Even when I was away in San Francisco, I loved it there, but it wasn't home. There was something about Portland that kept calling me, and it was only a matter of time before I listened.

The apartment seemed like a good omen. If Ollie was excited about it, then it couldn't be that bad of an idea. I would convince him. I had to. Ollie was a nomad at heart; he loved to travel and was always seeking adventure. Convincing him to leave San Francisco wouldn't be the hard part. Convincing him to stay anywhere for too long would be difficult, but even that wasn't what was worrying me. Convincing him it was a good idea for me to be in this city would be a monumental task.

He didn't make it a block from the apartment before saying, "Are you really sure about this?"

I sighed. "I'm *sure* I miss Portland."

"But are you sure you're ready?"

"I think so. I mean, I don't know that I'll ever feel *ready*, but I feel good about it. I mean, you saw that place; it screams Gollie, doesn't it?"

"Pulling out the 'Gollie', huh? You're that serious about this?"

I hated our ship name, the name some overly enthusiastic fans of mine had given us when Ollie started showing up in my videos. They assumed we were a couple, and no matter how many times I corrected them, no one believed me. Then I stopped correcting them. It was easier to let them think what they wanted, but I couldn't bring myself to get used to being referred to as 'Gollie'. Ollie loved it. The moment he saw it annoyed me, he decided it was the most hilarious thing in the world and used it as much as humanly possible. I hated the name, but I wasn't above using it to my advantage.

I nodded enthusiastically, feeling him cave a little. "I am. I'll let you call it 'Gollie's pad' or 'Gollie's garden' or 'Gollie G' or whatever you want. I'll even get a custom sign made or a doormat for right outside, so the whole world knows that Gollie lives there."

I saw the wonder in his eyes. "Anything else?"

"Whatever you want. You can have the better bedroom. You can have your pick of every dessert I get sent for a year."

His jaw actually dropped. I couldn't blame him. My fans were incredible and knew I had a bit of a sweet tooth. They were always sending sweets to me, and I very rarely shared them. Lately, Ollie was the only person worthy of me sharing with and even with him, I didn't share often. Before Ollie, I used to share them with Arty and Lanie. Arty would never ask, but I always shared with him. Lanie used to get jealous and sneak them when I wasn't looking. It was the only thing we used to fight about, and even then, the arguments dissolved into giggles quicker than the desserts could be eaten.

"You really are serious," he said in awe.

I nodded. "Whatever it takes. I need you, Olls. I want to come home, but I can't by myself. I mean, I suppose I could, but I know I wouldn't."

"I'll think about it."

"Thank you! Thank you! Thank you! You won't regret it!"

He chuckled. "I know I won't. I haven't agreed to anything yet."

He hadn't, but he may as well have. I knew him well enough to know that his agreeing to think about it was as good as him signing the lease with me.

"This calls for celebratory coffee! I know just the place."

I had been leading him toward Powell's City of Books, which was every bit as wonderful as the name implied, but a quick detour wouldn't hurt. It had been way too long since I'd had a good coffee.

It wasn't that San Francisco's coffee was bad; really, it wasn't, but Portland's was next level.

"I'm not really in a coffee mood. I could go for some tea, though."

"Absolutely not! You can't not have coffee on your first morning in the city. You haven't lived until you've had Portland coffee, trust me."

I knew he still didn't believe me until that first sip hit his tongue. When it did, he audibly groaned and immediately started chugging it.

I gave him a pointed look. "And you wanted to get tea."

He shrugged. "What can I say? When you're right, you're right."

"And?" I prompted.

He rolled his eyes and gave me a mock bow that made me giggle. "You were right, Your Majesty. Once again, the Queen of Cosplay can do no wrong."

We both laughed, and he offered me his arm. I looped my arm through his and immediately started humming "We're Off To See the Wizard", hoping Ollie would join. Not only did he join, but he immediately started belting the song. I started skipping. I couldn't stop myself. I dragged him a couple of steps while he grumbled about it before he picked up my rhythm and joined in. I couldn't wait to see what magic Powell's had in store for us.

Chapter Six

The moment we stepped into Powell's, I took in a deep breath and sighed. The smell of books and coffee made my heart sing. I was about to ask Ollie where he wanted to start before remembering he hadn't been here before. I looked over to ask him, but he had vanished. That was fast. I glanced around the entrance room for him and spotted his purple hair along the back wall, reading the blurb of a book. I was grateful he hadn't gotten far. With how big Powell's was, I probably never would have found him.

Powell's was big enough to be lost in for hours, if not days. There were numerous rooms, with bookshelves extending all the way to the ceiling and books crammed into every inch of shelf space. Once, on a bet, I had tried to count the number of shelves in the building, but gave up shortly after one hundred.

We never figured out who won that bet. Lanie got bored after fifty, and Arty stopped when I did. I was sure he would've kept going; he had an endless supply of patience, but Lanie and I wanted to buy our books and hurry home and he wasn't hard to convince. Things were simpler back then, back when I could count on Lanie and Arty to be on my side, have my back. I hated that things changed the way they did.

    Arty and I still talked every once in a while, but I hadn't talked to Lanie or the rest of our friends since I left. I missed the rest of them so much. I thought about reaching out to Sam, but I didn't want to make them feel like they were being put in the middle. I missed Eli dearly, but I wasn't sure he would answer if I reached out. He was really close with Lanie, and it would have hurt too much if he didn't answer, so I never tried. Ben would have answered, but I didn't know how to explain myself to him, because he would ask. He wouldn't sweep things under the rug with humor like Sam would, and he wouldn't try to be polite and pretend things weren't awkward like Eli would. He would flat out ask why I left them, and I couldn't tell them the truth. I couldn't face my out and proud friends and tell them the truth that I was still hiding from myself. I couldn't tell them the truth, but I also couldn't lie to them, so I didn't talk to them at all.

Arty was a different story. Arty already knew everything and was there for me regardless. I didn't deserve a friend like him, but I was grateful for his solid presence in my life. When we broke up, he made it clear that I would always have him in my life. He would always have love for me and would be there for me, however or whenever I needed it. Even at my best, he had always been too good for me. There was something inexplicably honest and pure about him. He was safe and comfortable in a way that I mistook for a long time for love. I loved him, but more like a best friend than romantically.

Even when I ended things, when I finally broke down and told him everything, he swore he would always be there for me. I hadn't believed him then, but he had been without fail.

I wished he was in Portland now, and I knew I would make plans to see him the minute he came back. It had been far too long, and I was excited to see him, but a part of me was worried. A part of me worried things wouldn't be the same, wouldn't feel the same. Of course they wouldn't. Our trio was now a duo, and I was on the outside. Things were back to how they were before I met them. It was Arty and Lanie against the world, and I was left adrift and alone.

Ollie called me, pulling my mind back from the dark place it was going. He rushed over with a book in hand and put his arm around me, pulling me close. I wasn't alone after all. Not really. I had Ollie. I couldn't imagine what I would've done without him, and I hoped I wouldn't ever have to find out.

As we browsed the shelves together, I felt at peace, more at home than I had in a long time. It was soothing being back in my favorite place, and I was happy to share it with Ollie. I was worried that I would be too haunted by memories to enjoy myself, but with Ollie there, most of them stayed away. I hoped as long as I avoided the second floor that things would stay that way. Ollie seemed to sense I was nervous about the stairs and didn't ask, just stayed with me on the first floor. I hated the feeling of weakness, but with Ollie's hand in mine, it didn't feel like I was weak. He brought out a strength in me. Made me feel less broken. I loved him fiercely for it and for how much he loved me.

In the gold room, with the fantasy books, I found Aggie's books. I picked up one of her stories, wondering if she had been here yet, but saw it wasn't signed. I would have to remind her to come here while she was in town. Aggie being in town was another big draw for me to come back, a big reason I didn't cancel coming home. I didn't want her to see me as weak or think any less of me. Although, I knew, deep down, that she wouldn't.

Aggie was one of my favorite people on the planet and loved me unconditionally. I missed her dearly and couldn't pass up an opportunity to see her. Even though she was my great aunt, I was closer to her than I was to a lot of my family. She and I were cut from the same cloth, two black sheep with our heads in the clouds in a family of white-collar professionals.

My parents didn't understand why I loved to cosplay, didn't understand my book obsession or my posting videos online. They didn't understand the community I had built for myself and the impressive, *overwhelmingly* massive following I had. But Aggie understood me. She had always encouraged my love of reading and was always gifting me books, whether hers or ones she enjoyed. I put her book back and continued browsing, hoping I would get to see her soon and wondering what she was working on next. I hoped she would give me something new to read, but until then, there were shelves full of books screaming to be read.

Chapter Seven

I could have spent hours there, but too soon, both Ollie and his stomach were grumbling. When I laughed, he gave me an exaggerated pout.

"I truly might perish. I might collapse in the middle of the store. You know what, continue ignoring me, it's fine. I'll be sure to haunt you."

"I can't imagine that would be much worse," I said with a giggle. "But fine, if you're sure you're too weak to carry on, we can go get something to eat. There's a cute cafe around here we can go to."

He perked up after that, grabbing my hand and pulling me to the exit. We were almost out when we both heard a voice yell, "BGC!"

My first instinct was to duck around the corner, but, of course, Ollie had slowed and was looking for the source of the voice.

"Come on," I whispered to him, gesturing with my eyes toward the door. "Let's go. I thought you were starving."

He grinned. "It can wait."

I rolled my eyes. He took a longer look at me and sighed. "I don't really know anyone here, Gwen. It might be nice to make some new acquaintances, especially if you're serious about moving back."

He knew I was. "If *we're* serious, you mean," I added.

He chuckled. "I'm not quite there yet."

"Don't worry, we'll get you there," I said, grinning.

My nerves spiked when I heard the voice getting closer. Ollie squeezed my hand. "Come on. I'm sure it won't be bad."

I sighed, knowing better than to argue once Ollie put his mind to something.

A curly haired, dark-skinned girl in a yellow sundress came bouncing around the corner. Ollie grinned triumphantly at how easy she was to find and stepped closer to her, getting her attention. "You're going to BGC, too?"

My anxiety lightened a little at her answering smile. She squealed, "New friends! Yeah, I'm in town for the ball. What about you both? Portland is beautiful!"

The look Ollie was giving me screamed, 'See? She's not so scary, right?'

I gave her a tentative smile.

"I'm Ollie, and this is Gwen."

"I'm Naomi! I'm glad I ran into you two! What are you both doing tonight?"

Before I could think of what to say, Ollie said, "Gwen here promised to show me around the city. She's from here. Are you going somewhere cool?"

"Yeah! I'm headed to Kennedy's with a group of people going to BGC. You both should come! Kennedy's used to be an old school building. Peak Portland vibes, if you ask me. Although I'm not local, so maybe I'm wrong?" She looked at me and paused.

"You're not wrong," I supplied.

"I knew it! That's the goal of this trip. Hit as many peak Portland places as possible."

Ollie elbowed me. "Sounds fun, right?"

I nodded.

"Say you'll come tonight. Pretty please!"

When I didn't disagree, Ollie grinned. "We'll be there."

"Can't wait! Now I just have to find where the rest of my friends wandered off to."

"We'll see you later," I said with a pointed look at Ollie. "Someone here is so famished he's on the brink of death."

Ollie laughed loudly, startling Naomi who laughed after a moment, too.

Before he could say or do anything else, I grabbed his hand and started to the door.

"I don't know what you were so worried about. She was nice enough," he said.

I knew he thought I was being dramatic, and maybe I was, but he didn't get it.

He didn't get the pressure that came with having a platform. The pressure to always be performing, the pressure to always be at my best, to always be perfect, the pressure to not disappoint anyone. The more people that followed me, the more people that adored me, the more I worried. The more eyes that watched me, the easier it would be to disappoint them. I hoped dinner tonight would be pressure free, but that was highly unlikely. I couldn't help but worry, but I knew it wouldn't be too bad. Come what may, at least I had Ollie.

Chapter Eight

Lanie

One day. She had a day left, and there was nothing about her dropping out. Nothing about her disappointing her thousands of fans, but nothing about her being in the city either. Her socials had all been cryptically quiet; I didn't like it. I wasn't one of her almost half a million followers, but out of desperation I had checked her socials. I hated myself as I did it, hated having to see her lying, gorgeous face. Even I couldn't find flaws in her appearance; it was her personality that let her down. It enraged me that people still couldn't see through her like I could, that people still took her side in what happened. Realistically, I should have been more forgiving of them. I was under her spell for a long time, too, but now that it was broken,

I hated her with a burning passion. Hated who she was and what she did to the man she promised never to hurt. She lied.

If I never saw her again, it would be too soon. My temper couldn't handle it. I wouldn't back down and I wouldn't be kind. I knew that much about myself. For Arty, I would try to ignore her, but I knew myself well enough to know I probably wouldn't succeed. Worse still, the way her followers stalked her like lovesick puppies, Arty would probably see anything that happened online before I even had a chance to tell him, a chance to explain.

That was why I couldn't have her here. I didn't want to disappoint him. She deserved worse than I would give her, but I didn't want to hurt him. I hated that he was worried about her, hated that he was still making excuses for her and still clearly cared about her. That pissed me off the most. After everything she did to him, I hated that he still cared, but I wasn't surprised in the slightest.

He was an eternal optimist and unwaveringly kind, which was why she never deserved him. That she had left him for *Lancelot* was a slap in the face. Okay, so I didn't actually know him, but from the little I'd seen in her videos, I wasn't impressed. Realistically, it wouldn't have mattered if he was a philanthropist billionaire by day and Batman by night; he wasn't Arty. Arty was worth a billion of any other man put together, and Gwen not knowing that made her not the girl I thought she was.

She wasn't the girl her followers thought she was either. If anyone truly knew what she was like, they wouldn't follow her, but four-hundred-fifty-thousand people still did.

With a sigh, I checked her socials again. Nothing. I huffed, shoving my phone in my pocket roughly. She was always on her damn phone. You would think she would be updating her followers about where she was like she always used to do. Now, the one time I needed her to post an update, she wasn't. She wasn't even good for that.

I tried to convince myself that no update was a good sign. Surely if she was back in Portland, she would update her socials, right? Surely if she was still going to Books, Gowns, and Crowns, she would post about it, right? The event coordinators brought her on as an influencer, so that must have been somewhere in the contract that she had to post about it, right? Maybe I was worried about nothing. Maybe.

A moment later, I couldn't resist pulling my phone out again. Maybe the website posted an update. I glanced at my lock screen, smiling at the picture of me and Arty with our arms over each other's shoulders in our armor. Things were simpler back then, back before Gwen stormed in and ruined our lives, back when it was only me and Arty. Before Gwen burned Camelot to the ground and danced on its ashes with *Lancelot*.

I did everything I could to pick Arty back up, to rebuild him and make him feel as confident as he had, but I knew he was hurting. She had been his life, and I hated seeing him hurt, hated that she wasn't hurting, hated that her following hadn't suffered at all but his had. When they split, people took sides and a good amount took Gwen's. To be fair, neither of them explained what happened, but people had their theories, and some of those theories were less than kind to Arty. He never refuted them and he never seemed to let it bother him, but I knew different.

He had a bright future ahead of him. He was working on building up his online following and carefully maintaining his image so he could run for State Senate next year. He had been dreaming of getting into politics for as long as I had known him, which was almost his entire life. I used to laugh that off, thinking he'd change his mind as he got older, but he never wavered. He was going into politics in one form or another. He wanted to make the world a better place, and I didn't doubt he could. He was optimistic to a fault and brought out the best in people. He made people want to impress him. He had a smile that made people want to listen to him, want to follow him.

He would be a great leader. He had his sights on State Senate now, but who knew what the future held. Even as a realist, I knew there wasn't much out of his reach. With his parents' financial backing, his own hard work, and his calling to change the world, I knew he was destined for greatness. If he wanted to go all the way to the White House, I didn't doubt he could. Whatever he chose to do, he would make a real difference, bring about real change.

The only problem was how trusting he was. He wasn't cut out for the political landscape, and try as I might, I couldn't shield him from everything.

The fallout from the breakup with Gwen couldn't have come at a worse time. He had been laying the groundwork for announcing his campaign run. If any of his followers paid attention, they wouldn't have been surprised, but he was excited to announce it. Then everything happened with Gwen and he lost a lot of his online following. It seemed like more of them were only following him to see her than I had thought, or more of them believed her lies than I thought.

They were supposed to be a power couple, a dynasty. A politician and a social media influencer with a big following, they were poised to be a force to be reckoned with.

A King Arthur and Queen Guinevere reborn and establishing their Camelot. Arty was destined for greatness, destined to rule, to lead, and he had wanted her at his side. It was the only bad decision I'd ever seen him make, and it cost him support and motivation.

He was brokenhearted and stopped working toward his goals. Only recently had he started to make moves toward that again, and I'd be damned if anything got in his way again. Nothing would. I would do what I failed to do last time and I would shield him from those who wished him harm. He was too good for this world, and anyone who couldn't see that was clearly blind.

She clearly hadn't seen it. If she did, if she knew his worth, she never would have left Arty for *him.*

I took a deep breath, running my fingers through my hair. She wouldn't be coming. She couldn't be. There was no way she would show her face after what she did. This was supposed to be our weekend; there was no way she would come.

I sighed and checked my phone again. No updates, but it was getting late, and I was meeting up with Eli soon. I would have to get going if I was going to make it in time. Eli's cousin was coming to town for the convention, and he was so excited for her to meet our friends. She wasn't from around here and he hadn't seen her in ages, so we were taking her to some of the big tourist spots. I didn't know when I'd be home or how long it would take, so I grabbed my long black coat on my way out the door. Whether it was the weather or the people, the one thing you could count on in Portland was unpredictability, so it was better to be prepared.

Chapter Nine

I rushed the entire way there, checking my phone every couple of minutes. I was late, and I knew Eli hated it when he had to wait. Today would be even worse, since he was itching to show Jade the city.

He talked a lot about her, but not in a way that made her seem like a real person. Right now, she was a bundle of odd facts, and I was curious to meet her.

Eli told me that as a kid they used to play make believe together. They were pirates searching for treasure, knights slaying dragons and rescuing princesses, mermaids swimming the seas and playing with dolphins. They were only limited by their imaginations, and he said hers was unmatched.

They used to take nature walks hunting for fairies. The most they ever found was a playful frog that Jade kissed. Jade ended up getting Salmonella, despite her protests that that was impossible because she had kissed a frog, not a salmon. She was in bed for a few days and kept insisting to be let outside to find her prince, because once the frog turned into a prince, he wouldn't know how to find her.

Shortly after, Eli's family moved away when his father got a job offer in Portland. They still talked pretty often, but Eli hadn't seen Jade in person since they were kids. When he heard about the ball, he thought of her and invited her immediately. It was a resounding yes.

At first, he was really excited, but the closer we got to the convention, the more nervous he got. He had been telling me weird things about her for weeks now. Not just me; all our friends. It seemed like he was worried she wouldn't fit in with us. When he found out she had made a few friends come, that helped him to calm down, but overall he was nervous.

I couldn't understand why for the life of me. I mean, this was Portland. We were used to weird. Sure, she didn't like open water because she worried about evil sirens or whatever else might lurk under the water, but it was natural to be afraid of the unknown. He said when she took walks in the woods, she would still leave little gifts for fairies, just in case. That was a little odd, but it was harmless. I couldn't understand why he was so nervous, but after hearing as much as I had about her, I was interested in meeting her.

I got to the coffee shop in record time. I drew in a few deep breaths, winded from practically running there, and opened the door. I sighed as I was enveloped by the sweet coffee aroma. I never tired of that. It was one of the many reasons Portland was the greatest place on Earth. There were so many unique coffee shops. It felt like you could live in the city your whole life and never run out of new coffee places to try. Although that might have more to do with the fact that once you found a favorite, it was hard to make yourself keep trying new ones.

I had been like that, but now I tried to explore a new place at least once a week. I was hoping to find one better than my old favorite, but so far, no matter how good the coffee was, it wasn't the same. So far, none had lived up to my favorite, desperate as I was to find a new one.

I hadn't gone there since *she* left us. It was her favorite place that she had insisted on bringing me and Arty to. I had been adamant that the place next to our apartment was the best, but she insisted on dragging us five blocks away even though there was perfectly good coffee on our block. She had insisted, and boy was she right.

When I tasted their coffee, I audibly moaned and my blood sang. As the amber liquid coated my throat, I knew I was in paradise. One look at Gwen and I could hear the 'I told you so' in her smile. Arty, Gwen, and I spent hours tucked into our favorite booth in the corner. That booth had seen some of our best moments and some of our worst, but now I steered clear of the place and was desperately chasing a substitute. In a city of coffee, there had to be another perfect cup somewhere else, but I hadn't found it yet.

This shop was Eli's favorite. Personally, I felt their blends were a little too bitter, but today wasn't about me, so we all agreed to meet there. I didn't know what the plan was for the rest of the day, but Eli had mentioned something about Jade wanting to go to Kennedy's. It made sense that she would want to see everything unique about Portland, and Kennedy's was certainly unique.

I looked around for Eli and was surprised to only see Sam's shaggy light brown hair and Ben's black hair peeking out of the beanie he was wearing. So much for having to hurry. Eli wasn't even here yet.

I waved to them and Sam nodded to me, but Ben was too engrossed in what he was saying to Sam to notice me. I ordered my regular and went to join them. I took a sip and sighed when it hit my tongue. It wasn't perfect, but coffee was coffee and I was happy. Today was shaping up to be a good day. I was spending time with my friends, exploring the city I loved. There were certainly worse ways to spend time. That and there had been no updates on Gwen being here, so it seemed like things might be going my way after all.

I joined them in time to see Sam rolling their eyes at what Ben was saying. I caught enough to hear that Ben was insisting that *Assassin's Creed Odyssey* was a superior game to *Assassin's Creed Unity* and couldn't help laughing. Sam grinned at me as I pulled out a chair and joined them.

Ben looked over, surprised for a moment, before saying, "Good, you're here. Now tell Sam why they're being incredibly dumb."

I chuckled. "I'd love to, but why exactly this time?"

Sam gave me a 'play along it'll be hilarious' look before saying, "I was just telling Ben here that while *Assassin's Creed Odyssey* is cool, clearly *Assassin's Creed Unity* was the better game."

Ben threw his hands in the air. "Honestly, man, I don't know how you can be so smart and say something so stupid. Tell them, Mor; they're clearly wrong."

I made a show of considering, deciding if I would play along. It was easy to get Ben worked up and hilarious to see Sam drive him insane. Normally, I stayed out of it, but I was in a good mood and Sam had a mysterious twinkle in their eye that had me curious.

"I'm sorry, dude, but I gotta give it to ya."

Before I finished, Ben crossed his arms triumphantly, giving Sam a look of superiority.

"See, I told you I was right. One game is clearly better than the other. Clearly *Assassin's Creed-*"

"Unity," I interjected. "Clearly, Unity is the better game."

Ben's jaw fit the floor as he looked at me in disbelief before throwing his hands in the air again. "I must be the only sane guy at this table."

With a chuckle, Sam added, "Well, you got part of that right."

Sam and I laughed hard. Ben looked between us, confused, "Part of it?"

Through my laughter, I said, "You're the only guy."

Sam laughed harder and Ben rolled his eyes. "I don't know why I put up with you two."

"Must be my dashing good looks," Sam supplied.

A voice from behind me said, "It's clearly your winning personalities."

Eli.

I turned around, grinning. "You're one to talk."

From behind him, a lilting voice added, "He's definitely one to talk. He never stops."

We all burst into laughter. I looked up and saw the voice came from a girl who had to have been Jade.

I was surprised to see that while she had the same fair skin Eli did, she didn't share his dark curls. Her hair was mostly straight with a slight wave to it, but it was a soft green. Her natural hair had to be a lot lighter than Eli's for her to have been able to achieve that color. I was surprised to notice that she was wearing a long, flowing skirt that matched the exact shade of her hair.

Her hazel eyes shined with her laughter. She looked around at us, and I waited for Eli to introduce her, but Eli didn't notice.

After another moment, I couldn't wait anymore. "Come on, man, you're supposed to introduce her." I elbowed Eli, who only laughed harder.

I moved closer to Jade. "Since Eli can't be bothered, I'm Morgana most days, Mor to my friends. This here is Ben. He's the brains of the operation. This is Sam, and we'll get this out of the way real quick, Sam's pronouns are they/them."

Sam nodded with approval. "As if I'd let myself be put into a box. It wouldn't be fair to the women or the men of the world to compare anyone to me."

"As you can see, Sam's self-esteem is clearly hurting," I said.

"If their ego were any bigger, it would need its own table," Ben added.

"What can I say? I know what I look like. If any of you looked like me, I wouldn't expect you to be humble."

Jade looked curiously at Eli, who was enjoying the show too much to say anything.

"Sam's messing with you, sort of. They have a big personality, but are incredibly kind and fun to be around."

Sam smiled, but Eli did a double take. "You're not getting soft on us, are you, Mor?"

I grinned. "Never." To Jade, I added, "I'm clearly the group's resident badass."

Jade looked at me appraisingly. "Noted, and where's the famous Arty that I've been hearing so much about?"

I frowned, but Eli jumped in. "Unfortunately, he's out of town. I would've loved for you to meet him."

"You would've loved him. Everyone does," I added.

"Too bad he's too busy visiting family," Sam said, adding with a bad British Accent, "across the pond." We all laughed. Their accent was so bad, you couldn't not.

Eli had had me worried about Jade, but she was fitting right in with us and didn't bat an eye at Sam's antics. Thankfully, since Sam wouldn't have been able to tone themselves down if their life depended on it. Even Ben, who was always going at it with Sam, loved Sam for Sam. Sam was unapologetically themselves and dared anyone to try not to like them, which was an impossible feat. Like Arty, Sam was charismatic, but unlike Arty, Sam basked in the attention.

Jade nodded to herself, giving a meaningful look to Eli. "You're right."

"About what?" I asked, but Eli just grinned.

"Told you so."

Sam, Ben, and I exchanged equally confused looks before Ben said, "Fine, keep your secrets." He glanced at his watch and asked, "So, where to?"

We all looked at Eli, who looked at Jade. "First stop is Voodoo, right?"

Before any of us could say anything, Eli added, "It's her first time in town, guys."

Before I could say it, Sam did. "We know, we know. You only reminded us twenty times each."

Eli chuckled and said, "Just wait until I tell you how we're getting there."

I looked down at the bike with a gulp. It couldn't be that hard, right? I had ridden a lot as a kid; it had to be the same now, right? After all, everyone always said you could never forget how to ride a bike. Living in Portland, I had already gone a criminally long time without riding a bike, but I was sure it would come back to me.

Eli and Jade were already off, with Ben close behind. It was only me and Sam now. I swung my leg over the bike, and it started to move. Sam's arm shot out and grabbed the handlebars, steadying it. *That can't be right.* How did everyone else make it look so easy? Then I noticed Sam's hand was holding the brake handle on my bike. *Of course,* I mentally berated myself. *How the hell could I have forgotten about the brake handle?* I gave them a small smile and positioned my hand where theirs was. I hoped they didn't know I wasn't confident, but their understanding look told me they did. Despite their bravado, they could be soft and caring when they tried. I hated being vulnerable, but they softened the embarrassment.

They glanced up, seeing the others waiting for us at the corner before stepping closer to me and saying "You got this. It's easier than it looks. Just make sure to hold the brakes when you're getting on, and remember the brakes if you're going too fast. As long as you're in motion, though, you won't fall."

I gulped, swallowing my sarcastic retort about how he made it sound so easy, and simply said, "Thanks. You're the best."

They watched as I mounted, making sure I was steady before doing the same. "Don't I know it," they said with a wink as we pushed off at the same time.

I held my breath, waiting for the bike to wobble under me, to show the others definitively that I didn't know what I was doing and was being bested by a bike, but it stayed steady as I pedaled. A small miracle, but a win was a win.

Chapter Ten

After Voodoo, all of us full on donuts, Eli decided on Powell's, but Jade wanted to go look at crystals. We had ridden by a shop she wanted to stop in on the way to Voodoo. I could tell Eli was going to protest, so I loudly reminded him that it was Jade's first time in the city. He chuckled and off we went.

I was happy to have time to prepare for Powell's. It wasn't that I didn't love bookstores, I did, but this *particular* bookstore was full of reminders of *her*. I didn't fault Eli for wanting to go there. When it came to showing Jade the city, there was only one bookstore that would do. Any local knew it was the best bookstore in the area, the largest independent bookstore in the world. There wasn't a substitute in the city, but facing the store this weekend in particular would be tough.

I had been there once or twice since, but it wasn't the same and I hated that. I hated that she ruined it for me. This weekend was meant to be a fun time with my friends and I didn't want to have to think about *her*. I didn't want to let her ruin it like she ruined so many other things. I could opt out and meet up with them later, but if I did that, she was winning. I couldn't let her win. I would have to go, and would have to get control of my emotions. I could do it. I could go there and not think about her. I could go there and enjoy myself like she never existed, like she never tainted the place with her memories. This weekend wasn't about us anymore, it was about me, and I was taking back my city.

Ben and I hung back while Eli, Jade, and Sam looked at the crystals. I was having a hard time getting out of my head, of not thinking about her. I had checked my phone a few more times to see if she was in the city, but there was no update.

I had been looking over my shoulder as we rode through the streets, scanning the area for her red hair. I didn't really believe she was coming, but that didn't stop me from holding my breath around every corner. I hated that she had me so on edge.

I tried to push her out of my mind and look at the crystals, but they weren't keeping my attention. I looked over at Ben and noticed he was on the move. Something had caught his eye, and, curious, I followed him. As we rounded the corner, I caught a glimpse of silver. I gasped, taking in the huge display of swords and daggers of all shapes and sizes hanging on the wall.

"Nice!" I exclaimed, clapping Ben on the back. "I need all of them, right?"

"I don't know how many you need but I know you can't have that one," he said, pointing to a gilded rapier.

I arched an eyebrow at him. "I can't?"

"Absolutely not. That one's mine. It's calling my name. You can have your pick of any or all of the others, but this one's mine."

I laughed, but surprisingly, Ben didn't.

"You know you can't ride around Portland with a sword on your back, right? We'd have to come back for it."

He looked thoughtful for a moment before saying, "I can't, but you could carry it for me."

"I'm happy you're admitting my superior strength, but no, I can't. Not without getting questioned by the police or something."

"Sure you can! You're half-white."

I rolled my eyes. I was half-white, but I was Filipino on my mother's side and looked more like her. A curse that I had been trying to escape since she kicked me out when I came out to her as a lesbian.

Ben was half-Japanese and half-black, but he had a much more loving family. They supported him when as a little girl he came out to them and wanted to transition. As much as he complained about his family, I made sure he knew how lucky he was.

I hadn't talked to my family in years. I would kill for a family like his.

"Only half, so only half the privilege. Besides, I doubt white privilege extends to swords in public."

I doubted even Portland was ready for the sight of a me, a six-foot-tall half-Filipino lesbian and Ben, a half-Japanese and half-black transgender man wandering the streets with swords. Adding in Sam as a non-binary Hispanic person, and Eli as a gay man, and we were a regular queer traveling circus. Even without the swords, we attracted attention.

He sighed. "Fine, but I'm coming back for it later."

I was surprised he agreed so quickly, but even here in Portland, you couldn't wander around with a sword.

Maybe I would come back with him later. There was a broadsword that was calling me. The polished silver hilt with an emerald inlay would have gone perfectly with my Cassandra armor. Unfortunately, the convention venue and the ball venue both had strict no weapons policies, so I would have to go without, but the sword looked like it was made for her. Maybe it was. Cassandra was a really well-known character, so it was possible. I leaned forward, trying to get a closer look, but I couldn't tell if it was her insignia.

I heard a cough behind me and whipped around to see Eli behind me with a smug look on his face. He was always so damn sneaky. I hated that I never heard him coming up behind me. I glared at him, but he just grinned.

"You guys are getting swords?"

"Ben might be," I said.

"Definitely am," Ben corrected.

Sam popped around the corner, with the others in tow. They took one look at what had our attention and announced, "That settles it. We're all buying swords, right?"

Eli laughed. "Speak for yourself. What would we even do with them?"

Sam shook their head, disappointed. They spoke at the same time that Ben did. "Sword fights, duh," they said in unison. Sam looked impressed and high-fived a surprised looking Ben.

"Come on, man," Sam added to Eli. "We'd be like real knights."

"The Knights of the Round Table," I couldn't help adding, looking lovingly at the swords.

Everyone except Jade groaned.

I blushed and saw Jade look around at them all, clearly confused.

"Mor's really into legends, specifically Arthurian."

Jade grinned. "I love those stories. Guinevere is my favorite."

Internally, I groaned. I tried to smile, but knew it looked more like a grimace.

Eli swooped in, saving me from replying, "Word of advice, cuz. Don't get her started on Gwen and Lancelot."

Jade looked at me, confused. "What's wrong with Gwen and Lancelot?"

I groaned again. "Only everything. Gwen was Arthur's Queen. She had a duty to him and her kingdom. He loved her more than himself and would have done anything for her. He literally gave her the world at her feet, his kingdom on a silver platter, and she broke his heart. She abandoned him and broke his trust to run off with Lancelot, of all people. Tell me, what's so special about that damned *Lancelot*? What did he have to offer that Arthur didn't?"

Jade looked thoughtful before saying, "Well, love."

"That's bullshit. Arthur loved Gwen with everything in him."

"That might be true, but if she didn't return those feelings, then no amount of love or self-sacrifice from Arthur could have changed that. No one wants to have to force others to see their value. Him and Gwen weren't right together, but that doesn't mean he doesn't get to be happy. He still deserves happiness."

"You're damn right he does! But how could he possibly be happy when she stole that from him?"

"She loved someone else. There wasn't any changing that or changing her mind. Would you rather she have gone on pretending?"

"She should have! For his happiness and for their kingdom, for the good of Camelot, she should have!"

"You would see her sacrifice herself for the kingdom?"

"Absolutely. Arthur and Camelot deserved better."

"What about Gwen?"

"What about her?"

"Doesn't she deserve to be happy?"

"Not after how badly she hurt Arty."

I didn't realize my slip until I took in Eli and Sam's expressions. She was talking in hypotheticals. I don't know when I let the conversation get away from me, but I hadn't realized it before I used Arty's nickname.

Before I could say anything else, Eli put his hand on Jade's shoulder and Sam put their arm around me. I tried to shrug them off, but they were persistent. They leaned into me, and I sighed, knowing it wasn't a battle I would win, so I let them stay there.

"It's a touchy subject," Eli told her.

Everyone knew that was an understatement, but it was enough. I was grateful when Eli quickly changed the subject. Unfortunately, his new focus was Powell's.

Chapter Eleven

As we dismounted our bikes at Powell's, I almost fell off mine when Ben loudly yelled from behind me, "You've got to be kidding me!"

I gripped the brakes hard enough to steady myself just in time, stopping myself from toppling over.

I looked back to see what he was upset about and saw him pointing at a woman across the street. She was in what looked to be some sort of cosplay combat leather outfit, but when I saw her, I knew at once that wasn't what Ben was talking about. He had to be talking about the large rapier she had strapped to her side.

I laughed. I couldn't help it, especially when he added under his breath, "And she's not even white!" The others looked confused, but I was laughing too hard to explain and Ben was too busy glaring at me to answer them.

Sam shrugged and ushered Jade inside, leaving me, Ben, and Eli to follow. I was glad Jade was going to get to see Powell's. It was a must see for any bookworm that came to town. I just didn't love that I had to see it with her.

It still held too many memories. I figured Eli knew that since he was hanging back by my side instead of showing Jade around. He was letting Sam take over the tour, which they were more than happy to do.

Ben took off for the Historical Fiction section and said he would meet up with us later. I watched Sam steer Jade to the romance, unsure if it was their idea or hers. Eli watched me a moment before asking, "Where to?"

I shrugged, not caring where we went. "You don't have to hang back with me. I'm not great company today. I'm sure you'd rather be with Jade."

"I'll have plenty of time to see her. No worries, man. I made you come in here, cause let's be honest, it was about time. A crime that you've been staying away for so long, but I won't make you face it alone. I'm here for you."

I smiled at that. I still wished Arty was here, or that I was literally anywhere else, but I appreciated the effort Eli was putting in.

"Fantasy?" I asked, and he quickly agreed. I knew that was the right answer, or at least that it was never the wrong answer. I wasn't looking for anything in particular, so I was happy to browse where he wanted, as long as we stayed away from a certain floor, but Fantasy was safe.

As we walked past the stairs, I averted my eyes, not wanting to look at or think about the last time I had walked them, about who I had walked them with. She might not have been dead, but she was to me, and just like the dead, she was haunting me.

When I couldn't avoid looking any longer, I could almost see her grinning at me over her shoulder, auburn hair bouncing as she ran up the stairs, racing me. I let her win. I almost always did. I wasn't usually competitive, but even if I had been, the way her smile lit up her face when she won, the way her laugh brightened my day, it was worth taking the loss, worth listening to her gloat. I knew Arty did the same. She almost never lost at anything. We never let her.

I hated that I couldn't stop seeing her everywhere. We turned a corner and I could have sworn I saw a girl with her hair, but when I turned back for a closer look, the girl had already gone around another corner. My heart stopped racing when the girl was gone, but I hated the effect that *she* still had on me. I hated that I was being driven mad by the idea of seeing her. She probably wasn't even in town. She would have been stupid to come, and she was a lot of things but stupid wasn't one of them.

Beautiful, brilliant, and deadly. A wolf in sheep's clothing. A cunning, heartless woman who didn't care who she hurt, but she wouldn't be stupid enough to show up here, especially with Arty away. There was nothing here for her anymore, and she didn't have the nerve to face me alone.

I held onto that, repeating it to myself like a mantra all afternoon while I browsed the shelves with Eli. I didn't buy anything, which was a miracle, but there were a few books I wanted to get tomorrow, so I was saving my money for those.

Eli and Ben were doing the same. Sam had said that was their plan, too, but I wasn't the least bit surprised when they showed up at our meeting point loaded down with books. I was surprised that Jade, who was trailing behind them, only had a single book in her hands.

When I looked at it, I was excited to see it was Cassandra and Ivy's story, a personal favorite of mine. I asked her about it and was a little disappointed to find out she hadn't read it yet, but I told her how great of a book it was and that she was going to love it and spent a while telling her about my cosplay, since she was kind enough to ask.

Surrounded by my friends, Powell's wasn't all that intimidating anymore. I handled Powell's, so I knew I could handle anything else that was thrown my way. She wouldn't show up, but if she did, I would be ready.

Chapter Twelve

Gwen

After lunch, we still had some time to kill before meeting with my great aunt Aggie so we went back to the hotel to relax a little and read. I had tried to tell Ollie we couldn't go to dinner with Naomi and her friends since we were meeting with Aggie for lunch, but he knew I was using that as an excuse. We would have plenty of time to do both.

I was nervous and excited to see Aggie. I couldn't remember how long it had been since I had last seen her, but I knew however long it had been was too long. We were kindred spirits, her and me, and she was one of my favorite people.

I was so excited she was in town for the convention. It was a big reason I found myself with the courage to come back.

She hadn't come to town for so long and now that she had, I couldn't miss her.

I was pumped she was going to get to meet Ollie, but she didn't know a lot about what happened between me and Arty, and I knew she would have questions. I was a little nervous about that. I wasn't really ready to talk about everything with her, but maybe now was the right time. She was only in town for a few days and was leaving before the ball, so I might not get another chance.

I hoped she could make more time for me, but I wasn't sure if she would be able to and who knows when I would see her next, so I had to tell her today.

I glanced at the clock again and saw only a few minutes had passed. I was supposed to be reading, but my book wasn't more interesting than the prospect of seeing Aggie again.

After the third time I looked at the clock, Ollie sighed, closed his book, and asked if I wanted to talk about it. I hesitated. I wasn't sure if talking about it would help or make it worse, but it was Ollie and I didn't keep things from him.

"I never told her why I broke up with Arty."

He looked surprised. Whatever he had expected me to say, it wasn't that. "You really didn't tell her?"

I shook my head.

"Why not?" he asked again. "Are you worried about how she might react?"

I shook my head quickly. That wasn't it at all. Aggie wasn't like that. I mean, she wrote queer books; I knew she wouldn't care, but that didn't make it any easier to tell her. It was one thing to tell your ex when you were breaking up with him to soften the blow, and to tell your queer best friend, but to tell Aggie made it real. Telling her was admitting to my feelings and admitting that I was holding back, that I wasn't living my truth. I prided myself on being honest and transparent. She always told me how proud she was of me for putting myself out there online to so many people.

I posted a lot of videos about my mental health and letting people know that it's okay to not be okay. I was authentically myself online, and admitting to Aggie that I was queer but not out felt like I was betraying my fans and myself.

I felt ashamed of myself for holding back, but I couldn't face the truth, not yet, because the truth would lead to more questions. If I told Aggie the truth, that I'm bisexual with a preference for women, then she might guess the truth about the breakup, that it happened because a certain someone caught my eye. That it happened because I fell hard for someone who wasn't Arty. That truth couldn't come out. I wouldn't be able to live with anyone knowing that. Arty was the only soul alive who knew that truth. Even Ollie didn't know who had caught my eye, just that someone had.

Arty knew the whole truth, and I don't know what I did to deserve that man, but he had been incredibly patient with me and faced all sorts of ridicule with all the rumors flying around. He gave me the grace and space to work through things on my own. As if I didn't feel terrible enough about what happened. He was literally the perfect man, even when being broken up with. He was caring, empathetic, and worried about me. I knew he had to be hurting, but he let me know he was more worried about me and that he would always be there for me.

If love was a choice, I would have chosen him. I wished I could have loved him the way he deserved. I would have been the luckiest girl in the world, but we weren't meant to be. I loved him in almost every way, except the way he deserved, the way a woman was supposed to love a man. He wasn't my *one,* no matter how much I wished he could be. He took the news better than I did. After the breakup, I had foolishly thought that maybe she would be the one for me, but I was clearly wrong. She didn't want anything to do with me.

I was still working through my feelings on everything, and letting Aggie have a glimpse into my mind right now felt like too much, but I didn't know if I could keep this from her. I didn't know if I wanted to.

Besides, I could really use her advice about how to tell the rest of the family. I knew she would be incredibly helpful with that, and I was getting to the point where I felt like enough was enough.

My family had never known why I left the city. Well, they knew I left after my breakup with Arty, but they didn't know why we broke up or why I felt like I couldn't stay in the city. It was hard to explain that without mentioning *her*, and since there was nothing that was ever going to even remotely happen with her, she wasn't worth mentioning. It would only hurt to bring her up, and I didn't want to keep reopening that wound. Too bad Aggie was incredibly perceptive.

I knew I had to come out to her; I wanted her to know the truth. She would be happy for me, and I needed that right now. I needed someone's positive reaction. I needed something good to come out of this weekend, and maybe it would give me the courage to come out to my parents and the rest of my family. My poor mother never understood why Arty and I hadn't worked out. She had loved him so much. Of course she did; everyone did. I didn't know what they would think when I told them. A part of me wondered if they already knew, but I wasn't sure they did. If they suspected, they hadn't told me.

I didn't know how to explain that to Ollie, but he cut in before I could start.

"If you're anything like me, you're holding back because telling her makes it feel more real, and telling her opens up questions you aren't ready to face yourself."

I stared at him. "How could you have possibly known exactly what I was thinking?"

"Easy. It's exactly what I've been thinking about."

Ollie was so confident around me and most people in his life that I always forgot that he wasn't out to his family. In fact, his family seemed to believe with the rest of the world that we were dating. I loved his family, and no matter how many times we told them we weren't together, they never seemed to believe us. It didn't help that we did everything together, but neither of us could bring ourselves to stop. He was my happiness, the light of my day, and there was no way I would stop spending time with him just because of some silly rumors.

"It's not easy, is it?"

"Not even a little," he agreed.

"Straight people have it so easy," I groaned.

"Well, at least there's a chance you might not have to deal with men," he said, laughing.

"Women aren't all that easy either," I said, thinking of a certain someone.

He got a serious look on his face, contemplated for a moment, and then nodded decisively. "Well, that settles it."

"Settles what? Huh?"

"Well, men suck and women suck, so we'll just be alone together. You and me, babe," he said, winking.

"Really, that wouldn't be so bad. Us together forever, and the first step is starting our new adventure in Portland, in our fancy new apartment."

He chuckled. "You think you're so slick sliding that in there, don't you?"

"I know I am. But tell me you can't see it, too? Us cooking together in that roomy kitchen, us watching movies cuddled up on our sofa, us stargazing from our porch. It would be like an endless sleepover, and you would get to enjoy my baking a lot more often."

He looked thoughtful before asking, "How much more often?"

I knew I had him with the baked goods. Ollie was easy to read, and even easier to bribe, especially when it came to baked goods. My followers sent me a lot of baked goods, but I had a knack for baking myself, too. There was something relaxing about whipping up the perfect dessert.

"Twice a week?" I asked.

"If you bump that up to three times a week, I'll sign the lease right now."

"Really?"

"Pinky swear."

I held out my pinky, holding my breath, thinking maybe he was messing with me, but he held his out, too. We linked pinkies and squeezed tight. After he let go, I tackled him with a squeal.

"I can't believe it! We're moving to Portland!"

He held me tight before saying, "You knew I was going to say yes eventually, but you brought up baked goods and I had to see how much I could get."

"Well, the joke's on you then."

"Why?"

"I would've agreed to five times a week," I said, and burst into laughter at the look of disappointment on his face.

"Wait, what?! No fair!" He tried to pull away, but I squeezed him tighter.

"It's not my fault you're a bad negotiator."

He chuckled. "You drive a hard bargain there, but I would've agreed without any baked goods. We both knew I was gonna cave. I've been looking for a new adventure, and Portland seems as good a place as any. I don't know if I ever told you I had been looking at places out here a while ago."

"What? No way! Why didn't you tell me?"

"Well, I was going to tell you, but then the breakup happened and you needed a place to lie low for a while, and things got complicated."

"Wait, no. Stop it. Don't tell me I ruined your plans?"

"I mean, no, you didn't. I didn't want to be here without you, and I knew you needed someone in your corner and I wanted to be that person for you."

I was tearing up. I couldn't believe he had kept that from me, or that I had gotten in the way of his happiness like that. Or maybe he was only trying to move to Portland to be closer to me, but something about the faraway look in his eyes told me that wasn't the whole story. I couldn't believe I had held him back and hadn't even known it.

"Wait, so what happened? Why were you moving in the first place?"

He hesitated, and I knew whatever was coming next was something he didn't want to say, or hadn't planned to say, anyway, and that it was going to be bad.

"Well, um, I wanted to be closer to you," he said, and I believed it was the truth. Well, part of it anyway, but it didn't feel like all of it, so I waited.

After a moment, he added sheepishly, "And there was a guy."

I gasped. "And you never told me?! What happened?"

He looked pained when he said, "It's a long story, but he wasn't thrilled I wouldn't come out to my parents and that I hadn't been able to come up and visit him yet. He started to think I wasn't actually into him. To be honest, I think he was worried I wasn't actually gay and that maybe I was just confused."

"But you were looking to move up here to be with him? That must've been really serious. I don't know why he wasn't able to give you more time to tell your parents."

Ollie hesitated again. This was going to be bad. I didn't know what he was still holding on to that he thought he couldn't tell me, but I hated seeing him upset.

"You know you can tell me anything, right?"

"I know, but this isn't your issue and isn't your fault, and I don't want you to feel like it is."

I gulped. "Just tell me."

"Well, when I cancelled my trip to Portland to meet him and look at places, he gave me an ultimatum."

"When was your trip?" I asked, pretty sure I already knew.

He didn't say anything.

Louder, I asked, "When was your trip, Ollie?"

He just frowned at me, and I felt my stomach drop. "No," I uttered, already knowing what he wasn't saying.

"But it's not your fault. That's why I didn't want to say anything."

"He gave you an ultimatum?"

He nodded nervously.

"What was it?"

"Well, he needed me to come out publicly. He wanted us to be together officially, like Facebook official and everything, super old school, but I couldn't do it."

"You weren't ready?"

He contemplated a moment before replying, "Well, yes and no. I wasn't ready, but I would have for him, but I couldn't."

"Wait, if you would have for him, why couldn't you?"

"Well, it was complicated. The timing wasn't right."

I watched him struggle with how to word what he wanted to say when the truth hit me like a freight train. It was my fault. The night Arty and I broke up, I was a wreck. Arty and I talked for a while, but I didn't feel good about dumping my emotions on to him. I had just broken up with him; it wasn't fair of me to expect him to sit there and listen to me cry about it, so I called Ollie.

We hadn't talked in a while. I had gotten distant from him when I was with my abusive ex. The asshole had made me distant from everyone, so I didn't feel like I had anyone to turn to about his abuse. When I finally got out thanks in part to Arty and Lanie, Ollie and I talked a little, but I couldn't bring myself to open up to him, to let him know what I had faced in silence.

I eventually told him, but not until after I got to San Francisco with him. But that night, even though we hadn't talked in a long time, I knew he would answer the second I called.

Him and I had met and bonded at a renaissance faire in San Francisco. I was invited there to cosplay with some of my online friends and he was working there for the summer. We hit it off quick and talked daily from that day forward until my ex started to get jealous. Until he forced me to cut everyone from my life, one by one. Ollie was one of the first to go. Even when I got out and was safe with Arty and Lanie, I was too embarrassed to admit what I had dealt with. Too upset at myself for letting him push people out of my life, so I stayed distant from Ollie.

Even though we hadn't talked in a long time, that night I knew it was him I needed to talk to. He was the only one removed enough from Arty and Portland that I could talk to about it. I couldn't talk to my new friends. They were all Arty's friends, too. They would have questions I wasn't ready to answer. My family was out, too, for the same reason. That left Ollie. I knew he would answer when I called and I knew he would be there for me without question or judgment, so I Facetimed him.

It rang a few times before he answered, and when he saw the tears on my face, he panicked and made me tell him everything. I did—well, almost everything—but I couldn't bring myself to tell him who it was that caught my attention. I wasn't ready to admit that to anyone, really. I had told Arty because I didn't feel like I could keep anything else from him, but I had barely just admitted it to myself. I wasn't ready to tell anyone else. I knew Ollie would support me without question and would let me open up about everything when I was ready.

I told him everything, everything except her name. I cried for a few straight hours, and he listened the entire time and was nothing but supportive.

He told I had a place with him for however long I needed if I wanted to come out and take some space from the situation. I thanked him, but turned him down. I told him I didn't know what I would do without him and that I loved him. That was when Lanie burst in.

I turned away from her, not wanting her to see my tears, but that wasn't what she was looking at. She was looking at Ollie on my screen.

She had stayed quiet for long enough for me to wipe my face and turn around. When I did, I was shocked to see she looked livid. I knew how much she loved Arty and that she would be hurt by our breakup, but I didn't expect anger. I was confused until she finally uttered words I'd never forget.

"I can't believe you were cheating on him. I can't believe you would do that. You're not the person I thought you were. You need to leave."

I was shocked. It took me a full minute to understand what she was saying; that she thought I had cheated on Arty with Ollie. It was ridiculous. Neither of us were even remotely interested in each other like that. I tried to utter some sort of defense, but Lanie wouldn't listen. She refused to even try to understand and just kept yelling at me to get out.

I finally agreed. If that was what she and Arty wanted, who was I to argue? Satisfied, she slammed my door on her way out and left our apartment, and I hadn't seen her since. Arty wasn't home, so I could only assume she was speaking for the both of them, so I packed up my things and left that same night. I got in my car and drove all the way through the night, only stopping when I got to Ollie's. I collapsed in his arms, and hadn't left his side since.

It wasn't until a few days later when I had the nerve to look at my socials that I realized the rumors Lanie was spreading about me and Ollie. It embarrasses me now that I felt a sense of relief at the rumors. I knew everyone would ask why Arty and I broke up. No one would understand, unless they guessed the truth that I wasn't ready to reveal, so I was relieved. Yes, some people thought I was a cheater, but I could deal with that. I wasn't ready to come out, and the rumors bought me more time.

I hadn't given a second thought to how the rumors might've affected Ollie. I had asked him, of course. I would have denied them if he had said he cared, but he hadn't told me. I should have known, should have asked more. He mentioned he had been talking to someone, and I never put two and two together.

"The rumors?" I breathed out.

He paused for long enough to confirm what I already knew before slowly nodding. "Since I wasn't officially out, and since you're-" I looked at him, confused before he continued, "You know, beautiful, stunning, a goddess on Earth…" I rolled my eyes. His smile faded when he continued, "Well, he believed the rumors. I tried to explain to him that things weren't like that, but he wouldn't listen, especially after he found out you were staying with me indefinitely and that I had halted my plans to move to Portland."

I started to interject, but he shot me a look. "Don't suggest for one second I could have or should have left you alone in San Fran without any friends or any place to stay. You would never do that to me and I wouldn't do that to you, but he couldn't understand that, and I don't blame him. Obviously, you and I aren't together, but I picked you over him. It wasn't even a choice, not really. You needed me, so of course I would be there for you. He couldn't understand that, and while I don't blame him, it clearly wasn't going to work out if he couldn't respect our friendship."

I didn't know whether to laugh or cry. A strangled noise halfway between came out of my throat, and Ollie pulled me to him and held me.

I took a few deep breaths, willing myself to not cry, but I knew it was a losing battle.

When I pulled away, Ollie brushed the tears from my cheeks and booped my nose, making me giggle. "Come on. It's not all bad. We have each other."

"And what a pair we make, sad and lonely, but at least we have each other." I couldn't believe he didn't resent me. He should resent me.

"At least we have each other," he agreed, his voice full of sincerity that made my heart break.

I vowed then and there I would do everything I could to make sure I helped him find happiness again. If I couldn't be happy, at least I could make sure he would be.

Chapter Thirteen

I was almost bouncing with excitement by the time we got back to the coffee shop cafe. It was my favorite and nothing less would do, even though I didn't exactly welcome the memories it held.

I let my gaze linger on the back booth for a moment, before turning my attention away. Today was going to be a good day. I was seeing Aggie today and nothing was going to sour that.

We ordered and were just sitting with our drinks when I saw her.

I squealed and jumped out of my seat, raced over to her, and wrapped her in a hug. She laughed when I squeezed her. "Easy there, dear. I'm not as young as I used to be."

I laughed and pulled away. "You don't look a day over 50."

"And that's why you're my favorite," she said, laughing. She noticed Ollie before I remembered to introduce them. "And who's this cutie over here?"

"Ollie, ma'am. Pleased to meet you. I've heard so much about you."

She waved a hand at him. "Knock it off with that ma'am stuff. Any friend of Gwen's is a friend of mine. It's Aggie, and get over here."

He grinned as she pulled him in for a hug.

I knew she would love him.

Once she got her drink and sat down, she gave me a look that I knew meant we were going to get down to business. I was nervous, not sure I was ready, but it felt like it was now or never and I knew I was safe with Aggie.

She looked between us and said, "So are my readers right?"

Ollie and I exchanged a confused glance. "Right about what?"

She gestured between us, asking hopefully, "Are you two an item?"

Ollie laughed loudly, and I blushed. "An item? No one says that anymore."

She waved her hand. "An item, together, doing the beast with two backs, whatever the kids say nowadays."

I burst into laughter, and Ollie nearly fell out of his chair.

"I'm not an expert on the kids, but I don't think they're bringing back Shakespearian phrases."

She chuckled. "Fine, but quit avoiding the question."

I shook my head. "No, we're not. Despite what everyone has been saying, we're just friends."

She looked between us, shooting a questioning look at Ollie, who nodded. "Well, that's a shame," she said, looking at Ollie. "He's a cutie."

Him and I laughed, but she looked back at me and asked, "But are you happy?"

I thought about that for a moment, probably longer than a genuinely happy person would have. After a moment, I gave her honesty. "I'm getting there. Some days are harder than others, but I'm a lot closer than I've been in a long time."

"Well, that's all I can ask for, then. That and that the moment there's someone special in your life you let me know."

"You'll be the first."

"Hey!" Ollie exclaimed.

"Okay, fine," I amended. "You'll probably be the second. I do live with Ollie after all."

She adopted a look of hurt for a moment before cracking a grin. "As long as I'm close to the top of the list."

"Always."

"Speaking of you two living together, I haven't asked in a while. What's your plan? Are you staying in San Francisco? I know you like it there, but I know how much you love Portland. I'm surprised you aren't itching to get back."

"Well, actually," I said, grinning.

"Wait, no!" she exclaimed, clapping her hands together in her excitement. "Did something happen with that Arty boy?"

My face fell for a moment. "Arty's a long story, but no, nothing's really changed. We're friends, though, which is more than I can say for Lanie and I."

"That girl was always a hurricane."

"You can say that again," Ollie chimed in. "A bulldozer, a wrecking ball. I have a lot of choice words for her."

I blanched. Yes, things had gotten bad, and yes, she hated me, but I still cared about her. One look at Ollie and he put his hands up in defense, offering an apologetic smile. "Sorry." To Aggie, he said, "Your niece isn't fond of me 'expressing my feelings' about Lanie."

"Yeah, because your feelings are often dramatic, loud, and highly inappropriate." He went to argue, but I continued, "Especially in calm public places like coffee shops."

"Point taken," he said after glancing around.

"So, if it isn't about Arty, what's going on?"

I smiled again. "Well, Ollie and I have been talking about moving back here."

"And by talking, she means she's holding me at knifepoint to sign the lease," he lamented.

Aggie grinned proudly, "That's my girl."

"Bribing with baked goods is hardly holding you at knifepoint."

"Well, you're definitely threatening to harm my waistline."

We all burst into laughter. Aggie regained her composure first and said, "I'm so happy for you, for you both. So, tell me, what else is new?"

The server came over with our sandwiches and as we ate, I talked to her for a while about my social media achievements. Then when I ran out of things to talk about, I talked to her about the other authors attending the signing the next day and asked her who she had met and who she thought I should read. It was a stalling tactic, and I knew from Ollie's pointed looks and him squeezing my thigh under the table that he understood and was here for me, however long it took.

I didn't know if I was ready, but it felt like if I didn't do it then, I never would. Aggie was in the middle of talking about an author she had met at her hotel that morning when I blurted out, "Auntie, I'm bi."

She paused mid-sentence and stared at me. I felt Ollie's fingers interlace with mine and squeeze, but I couldn't stop looking at her. It felt like time had stopped, but I knew it had only been a few seconds before her expression turned to confusion.

"Did you want me to set you up with her?"

Now it was my turn to be confused. "Her who? What?"

"Sadie, the queer author. She's quite pretty, too, might I add."

"What? Why?"

"Well, you loudly told me you're also into women when I was talking about her. I figured that meant you're interested?"

"What? No. I mean, maybe? I don't know. I don't know the girl, but this isn't about her, it's about me. You don't care?"

"Of course I care, darling. I just have known for quite a while. I thought you were a lesbian, though, so I had that part wrong. I was waiting for you to tell me, when you were ready, of course."

"You knew?"

"Of course I did. I'm a writer. We have an eye for these things."

"So you really don't care?"

"Of course not, sweetie. The only thing I care about is your happiness, not who makes you happy."

I felt myself breathe a big sigh of relief and broke into a grin.

She looked concerned. "Did you think I would care?"

I shook my head immediately. "No! I mean, yes. No. I mean, maybe? I don't know. I knew you wouldn't be bothered by it, but I haven't come out to many people; really only you, Ollie, and Arty. Coming out to you makes it more real. It's like I'm admitting to myself that it matters. I'm admitting to myself that I really do prefer women, that I want to date a woman, that I'm much more attracted to all women than I am to men. You had that part mostly right. I might as well be a lesbian."

She reached across the table, taking my other hand and squeezing. "Honey, I'm honored you told me, and so proud of you. I hope you know how proud."

I was tearing up and couldn't stop smiling. I couldn't believe how easily that had gone.

"Thank you so much. I appreciate you and love you.

"Both of you," I added to Ollie, squeezing his hand.

"So," Aggie asked with a mischievous look in her eye, "are there any special ladies in your life?"

I shook my head, willing my thoughts to stay away from *her*. "No. It's just me and Ollie."

"Really?" she asked.

I hesitated. "Well..."

Ollie perked up. "Well?" he asked, wiggling his eyebrows at me. To Aggie, he complained, "I've been after her for weeks for any sort of news, any gossip, anything, and she kept telling me nothing was new, and now all of a sudden there might be something to share? Aggie, where were you weeks ago?"

I blushed. "It's not news. I'm not ready."

Him and Aggie exchanged a look before Ollie connected the dots. "Ohhhh, the mystery girl."

I nodded, and Aggie looked intrigued. "There's a mystery girl?"

Ollie's eyes widened. "That's right; you have to catch her up on the breakup."

"Long story short, Arty and I broke up shortly after I realized I was more attracted to women. He was great about it, too good, really. He's ridiculously sweet about everything, and still checks up on me."

"What I wouldn't do for a man like that," he said wistfully.

"Honey, you're preaching to the choir," Aggie said. Ollie reached out and high-fived her waiting hand.

"Anyway," I said, getting back on track, "it wasn't just something I realized out of nowhere. There was a girl."

"Ahhh, the mystery girl," Aggie said.

I nodded, and Ollie groaned. "Don't think you'll get it out of her, though. I've been trying for weeks. Whoever it is must be really special."

"She is," I said sadly. "Unfortunately, I have no chance with her."

"Well, why not?" Aggie asked. "She's a fool if she doesn't see your value."

"Agreed," Ollie said. "My best guess is that she's straight."

I hadn't told him anything about her because I didn't want the questions or the judgment. She wasn't straight, but she might as well have been for how unattainable she was to me.

I just shrugged.

Ollie threw his arms in the air and gestured at me. "You see what I have to deal with? She tells me nothing."

I rolled my eyes. "You would think gossip was his life force."

He laughed. "It might as well be."

"Well," Aggie said, looking at me sympathetically, "if there ever is anything you need to talk about, you promise me you'll let me know, okay?"

She didn't have to elaborate for me to understand what she was saying; that she was asking me to promise not to hurt on my own anymore. She was still healing from my abusive relationship before Arty—so was I, to be honest—but when she found out I had suffered the abuse in silence, I knew she took it hard.

She asked me a few times why I didn't come to her, but I didn't feel like I could go to anyone. He made me feel alone and unlovable, like his abuse was my fault. I felt embarrassed and hadn't been able to open up to anyone about it, until Arty and Lanie. Until it got really bad.

They saved me, the two of them. They were there when no one else was. I wouldn't let anyone else in, but there was something about Arty and Lanie that demanded I let them in, demanded I let them love me how I should be loved, and once I did, I never looked back.

I hated that I had let myself be hurt and pushed around for so long in silence, but it wasn't something I would ever repeat.

"I promise. I know you're there for me."

"Whether you like it or not. What else are great aunts for except to be a great pain in your ass?"

All of us laughed hard at that.

When I caught my breath, I told her, "You're not a pain. Thank you for being here for me, both of you," I said. Then, looking at Ollie, I added, "Although you are a bit of a pain."

"Hey!" he exclaimed, elbowing me.

I bent over, laughing.

Aggie smiled. "I'm glad to see you're in great hands. You take care of her now, dear."

Ollie sat up straight in his chair with his chest puffed out in pride. "Absolutely."

They shook on it, and I couldn't help rolling my eyes even as a grin broke over my face.

"I can take care of myself, you know."

"Don't I ever," Ollie said.

"You take after me that way," Aggie said with a proud grin.

I hadn't felt so surrounded in love in a long while and I didn't want to leave, but Aggie had plans and we had a dinner to get to. I was thrilled I would at least get to see Aggie at the signing the next day, but hoped she would have more time in town after.

Now that I had come out to her, I was dying to get her advice on how and when to come out to the rest of the family, but it could wait. I was too nervous about dinner to focus too much on that looming task. I just wanted to celebrate my first victory, and I hoped dinner would go well, too.

Chapter Fourteen

Lanie

The whole time while getting ready for dinner with Jade's friends, I had a weird feeling that I couldn't shake. I felt like I should probably just stay home. Not that I didn't like Jade. I did. She was nice enough, and not nearly as eccentric as Eli had warned us all about. She fit right in with us.

I assumed her friends would be a lot like her and we would get along fine, so I couldn't figure out what was bothering me.

I pulled out my phone and, out of habit, checked Pendragon's socials. Still no update. I should've known since there hadn't been anything for the last few days.

I knew it was a good thing. If she were here, she would definitely post about it, but it felt too easy. It was unnatural that she hadn't posted in so long. She was being too quiet, too absent, and it was worrying me.

It felt like the calm before the storm, like she was planning something. I hated not knowing, hated the worrying, but if she was planning something, I was right to be worried.

Rationally, I knew she wouldn't go after Arty. She had no reason to and never had, even in the beginning, but I still worried for him. With her large follower count, most of what she did affected him. It didn't matter if she intended to or not, her followers were ruthless to him.

He believed it wasn't her fault, but he always saw the best in people. He never saw her clearly, never doubted her, even after. His unwavering faith and loyalty made me love him, but killed me when he directed it to her. She didn't deserve it. She had only ever used him, and now I was worried she was gearing up to do something big and I hated being at her mercy, having to wait to find out what it was.

I hoped I was wrong, but swore to myself that if she found a way to get to him again, I would make her pay.

I refreshed one more time, but no updates. With that, I shoved my phone in my pocket, grabbed my coat, and was out the door.

Chapter Fifteen

Gwen

I was having a good time and actually making new friends. Ollie kept shooting me 'told you so' glances and I couldn't blame him. Like usual, he was right. I was having fun and I really shouldn't have been so worried.

So far, there were two tables, with a third still empty. I hadn't met the girls at the other table yet, but I really liked the girls I was sitting with.

Naomi was super nice, and so were the others. Ollie and I were sitting with her, Skye, Erin, and Courtney.

Skye had brilliant blue, wavy, shoulder length hair that contrasted starkly with her fair skin. She was incredibly friendly, and her personality was as electric and vibrant as her hair.

I noticed Courtney's freckles and hazel eyes immediately. She had a great sense of humor, an accent I couldn't place, and a contagious smile.

Erin was a tall brunette with shoulder length hair. At first, I was worried she didn't like me, not because of anything she did, but because she was harder to read than the others. She was quieter and seemingly more observant. I worried she felt uncomfortable, but the second the conversation turned to her favorite book, she had more to say than anyone.

I couldn't deny it. I was actually having fun, but I should have known that wouldn't last. It was then that I noticed another group coming to join our party. I knew from what Naomi had said that we were probably waiting for more people, so that wasn't surprising, but when I turned to look at the newcomers, my heart stopped.

It was *her*.

I panicked. *I can't do this. I can't do this.*

I knew I was going to have to face her at some point, but I wasn't ready, not tonight.

I looked a moment longer, seeing that the whole crew was with her. Well, the whole crew except Arty. I gulped. I didn't know if Eli, Sam, and Ben would be enough to keep Lanie on her best behavior, enough to keep me safe.

I shrunk down a couple of inches, and Ollie followed my gaze and saw her. He immediately wrapped his arm around me and pulled me into him, shielding me and hiding me from view.

Thank goodness for Ollie. I don't know what I would have done without him.

I could hear the others at our table still talking and I winced, hoping I wasn't making too much of a scene, but I couldn't move. I couldn't face her here and now. I thought I would be ready, but I wasn't. I hadn't expected to see her here, and if I made it through tonight in one piece, maybe I would be more prepared to see her tomorrow, maybe, but I hadn't thought for a second that she would be coming tonight.

What were the odds? The universe must have found this hysterical. My heart ached just looking at her. I don't think she noticed me yet, but I knew when she did, there would be nothing but hatred in her eyes, and I couldn't stand the thought of that.

The last time I saw her was still burned in the back of my mind. She trusted me and she felt like I betrayed her. I had hoped that since Arty forgave me and had the grace of understanding that she would, too, but I should have known better. Arty was the best of us, and Lanie wasn't nearly as forgiving.

This was the first time I had seen her since that night, and the old wounds started to open. I felt the tears starting to pool in my eyes and tried to hold them off. I knew Lanie well enough to know that that would only make her more angry, and I didn't want to put Ollie in her crosshairs. I didn't want Ollie to see me suffering. I had to be brave; if not for me, then for him. He came all this way with me to ensure I had a great weekend and that I could enjoy myself. I didn't want his efforts to be in vain. In his arms, I felt safe. Despite knowing Lanie was only a few feet away, being wrapped in his protective arms, I felt like I could breathe, like things might be okay.

He squeezed me and rubbed the top of my head soothingly. I hoped he knew how he was single-handedly responsible for my sanity right now. He had saved me back then when I had nowhere else to go and no one to run to. Well, I had people I could have gone to, but no one that would have understood without question. No one that wouldn't have asked questions about Arty. No one that would have taken me in without hesitation like he had. He had saved me then, and he was saving me now. My knight in shining armor.

I gulped, thinking of a certain someone and her shining armor. I pushed the thoughts from my mind. Now wasn't the time or place, though I didn't think there ever would be one.

A moment later, everyone at our table went quiet. I froze, holding my breath, waiting for the inevitable.

"Hi."

Just a single syllable, but it was enough for me to know it wasn't Lanie, enough for me to start breathing again.

I was surprised that it wasn't Sam, Eli, or Ben either, though. I thought that maybe one of them would have come over to say something. Maybe not Ben, but Sam or Eli. On second thought, as much as it hurt, maybe Eli was too close to Lanie to think he should come talk to me. That stung a little, but I had to understand. They didn't get it. They would all have questions, and I couldn't blame them. I could only hope they didn't hate me as much as Lanie did.

Even if Eli didn't come over to say anything, I hoped Sam would. Sam had been the closest to me of the rest of the bunch. They had taken me in without question. Everyone had, but Sam was as enthusiastic about it as Lanie and Arty were.

I missed Sam dearly, but I hadn't had the nerve to reach out when I left, and after all this time, it felt like it had been too late. Sam could have reached out, too, but it wasn't on them to do it, and I knew that. I was the one who broke up with Arty and left town without saying goodbye to any of them. I couldn't blame Sam, or any of them, if they hated me like Lanie did.

Maybe I would be brave and approach them later. Maybe. I thought about facing Lanie of my own volition and shuddered. *Okay, maybe I could wait until Lanie went to the bathroom and approach the others then,* I amended. I knew I could never approach them while Lanie was there. I didn't have the guts for that.

But if the voice didn't belong to any of them, who did it belong to?

I freed myself from Ollie's grip, pulling back enough to see who it was. I didn't recognize her, but she was staring right at me. I blinked a few times, trying to clear the tears that were threatening to fall, and thankfully succeeded.

No one had said anything to her, and she was staring at me like a deer in headlights. I was certain I looked the same. I didn't know why she looked so startled, but I wanted to make her feel more comfortable, and she was staring directly at me.

I said the only thing that came to mind, "Hi."

She smiled gratefully, and I tried to smile in return, but it felt false. I hoped it looked more genuine than it felt.

She turned her gaze to the others and continued, "Hi, guys. I just wanted to come over, say hi, and introduce myself. Since I've already said hi, I should probably get to the introducing." I laughed a little at first, and then a little harder when she laughed at her own joke.

A moment later, she continued, "I'm Sadie Hawthorne, one of the authors for the event. You may or may not have heard of me. Probably not to be honest, but I wrote a queer feminist Sleeping Beauty retelling and a queer feminist Beauty and the Beast retelling. If any of you have read them yet, I'm sorry for the ending and I promise the next one is coming soon."

I laughed, and saw the others were smiling and was happy when they asked her about her stories. I didn't know her, nor had I heard of her, but I already knew enough to know I liked her. She seemed like my sort of person, and more than that, she somehow knew that I needed a distraction right now, and I was incredibly grateful for that. I knew I was going to have to look into her books later. Anyone that willingly stepped in between me and Lanie would have my undying loyalty. Not that she knew what she was stepping into, but I wanted to support her, anyway.

I didn't say anything, just listened as she weaved tales of daring heroism and women that didn't let society dictate their actions or their hearts. She wrote strong women who sometimes loved women and who were always true to themselves. I loved the sound of that.

That was who I wanted to be. I wished I could be stronger. A stronger person would have told their truth ages ago. A stronger person would have told Lanie the truth, the whole truth, but I wasn't strong enough then and I certainly wasn't now, not with the memory of how she had looked at me when she found out I had broken up with Arty still fresh and painful. Not with how angry she still was. I didn't think I would ever have the courage. I felt I could tell the whole world before telling her. That was terrifying, but it was far less scary than facing her and telling her.

The conversation moved on to retellings in general, and I wasn't surprised when a few minutes later, they mentioned

Aggie. She was a household name for a reason, but it warmed my heart every time I heard someone praise her.

I was surprised when, a moment later, Sadie slid in next to Ollie. I felt him stiffen, but he didn't say anything. I was thankful for that. I liked Sadie and was happy to have another person between me and Lanie.

When Sadie leaned closer to Ollie and motioned me to move closer, I did without hesitation, curious to see what she had to say. Even more curious, since she didn't seem to want the others to hear. I leaned over, but she didn't move any closer, so I leaned across Ollie's lap to get closer to her. I was practically sitting in Ollie's lap, but that wasn't unusual for us.

She moved to my ear, and whispered loud enough for me and Ollie to hear, "I'm so sorry. I know you don't know me. I just wanted to make sure you knew Morgana seems like she's on a warpath."

It took me a moment to register Lanie's newest name. When I knew her, she went by Ash to the public. I had heard a while ago that she had a new name, but had forgotten it. I almost rolled my eyes at how hard she was leaning into Arthurian legend, but I wasn't surprised. Lanie loved the Arthurian stories almost as much as she loved Arty himself. What did surprise me was that she went with Morgana instead of Merlin, or one of Arthur's many knights. Anyone else, short of Lancelot himself, would have made more sense to me, but Morgana was a strange choice.

Who Morgana was varied highly between stories. In some stories, she was Arthur's sister, in others, she held no relation to him. Sometimes she was his right-hand woman, other times she seemed to only serve herself. In some of the stories, she hated Gwen with a passion, but in others... I blushed just thinking about some of the stories I had read about how heated things got between Morgana and Gwen.

Lanie was headstrong, but choosing Morgana was calculated. I just couldn't work out why she would have chosen Morgana in particular. Maybe because of the strong hatred she possessed for Gwen in some of the stories, but it seemed to me Merlin would have suited those purposes as well. Although the more I thought about it, the more it made sense. Merlin seemed more detached in his hatred of Gwen. He hated her, yes, but not because of her per se, but because of what she represented and what she was prophesied to do. With Morgana, it had always been more personal.

Sadie had paused a moment, and I met her eye again, feeling guilty I hadn't given her my full attention before. I replayed her words in my head, 'Morgana seems like she's on a warpath'.

Not surprising, but not ideal either.

Sadie kept going. "I came over here to try to divert her attention from you."

Sadie looked over her shoulder. I followed her gaze and gulped, seeing that Lanie was making a beeline toward us. *Morgana*, I corrected. She was going by Morgana now, and I knew she used to hate when Arty or I called her anything except Ash in public, so I needed to remember and respect that. She was Morgana now; Ash and Lanie had both died that night, and I would do well to remember that.

Sadie looked stricken when she looked back and added, "But I guess it didn't work. I'm so sorry, but I promise you I'm not moving and you know Ollie isn't either."

I just stared at Sadie, stunned. I knew rationally that she must have been a follower of mine, but it always startled me when someone knew so much about me when they first met me. With Sadie, what stunned me the most was the confirmation that she knew who I was and who Morgana was and had still willingly put herself in between us. She didn't know me, not really anyway, and she didn't owe me any loyalty. She knew what she was putting herself in between and was still here. I was incredibly grateful to her. My heart soared at her kindness. She had just gotten herself a new fan for life. I would have to buy every book she had ever written from now until the end of time to repay the kindness she was showing me, and even that I didn't feel like would be enough.

She settled in as best she could and we all waited with bated breath for the oncoming storm. Morgana closed the distance and stood imposingly at the end of the table, looking down at us with hatred burning in her eyes.

Any words I might have been planning to say died on my lips at the force of her glare.

"Pendragon," she ground out.

If it had been anyone else who'd spoken, I could have laughed. I wasn't used to anyone calling me that. It was always Gwen. Yes, I cosplayed Guinevere Pendragon, but I always went by Gwen. I wasn't 'Pendragon' any more than she was 'La Faye'.

Hearing her address me as anything other than Gwen hurt, but having her use my cosplay last name was jarring. She knew my actual last name and could have used that. Even now, a small part of me found amusement at how far she was leaning into Arthurian legend.

"Lancelot," she said, looking at Ollie.

That stopped my thoughts in their tracks. I knew what she thought about mine and Arty's breakup. I knew what the world thought about it, but to hear her confirm that in public, after all this time, hit hard. I hated that she was dragging Ollie into this, and hated that anyone thought that the breakup was his fault. He didn't seem to mind since it let him protect me, but I hated it enough for the both of us.

I almost said something to defend him, but she continued before I could. "Didn't expect to see you here. I didn't know you'd taken things so public," she said, gesturing at us.

I was confused for a moment and looked at Ollie. Only then did I remember I was practically in his lap. I blushed at that. I felt my phone vibrate in my pocket. At least I think it was mine. It could have been Ollie's. I could feel his in his pocket, too. I would have to check it, but now clearly wasn't the time.

Ollie had his eyes on me, searching mine. Whatever answers he was looking for, he seemed to find, since a moment later, he nodded and turned to Larie. "Morgana, is it? At least I think that's what you're going by these days. Fitting since she was a nasty, conniving sorceress who didn't give a damn about anyone except her precious, perfect, could-do-no-wrong Arthur."

I almost gasped. I hadn't wanted things to turn out this way. I had wanted to be civil. I was shocked Ollie had pulled the first punch, but then again, I shouldn't have been so surprised. He was unfalteringly loyal to me and had seen how much of an effect Lanie had had on me. I had fled the city, my home, rather than face her. It was no wonder he didn't like her and was standing up for me, but he shouldn't have dragged Arty into it.

The words left my mouth before I could register them. I quietly told him, "Leave Arty out of it." It wasn't by far my only objection, but the only one I could find the words to voice.

Unfortunately, judging by the shade of red Lanie had turned, I hadn't been quiet enough. Although, what she could possibly have been upset about by me defending Arty, I didn't understand. I didn't have to wait long to find out.

"You don't get to call him Arty," she ground out. "You lost that privilege the second you became a cheating hoe and left him."

I shrunk down further. I knew how she felt already, but hearing her confirm my worst fears, so harshly and so loudly in public, made me want to sink into the floor and never resurface. I hated that we were having this conversation, hated how it was going, but hated even more that it was in front of these people that I had hoped might become my friends.

I didn't have a response. I just wanted this all to be over. I wanted to escape with some of my dignity, but Ollie didn't stay quiet. "I know you're not talking about Gwen like that."

I interjected, trying to get him to stay quiet so she would go away. "It's okay, Ollie. I'm not guilty in the way she thinks, but I know I hurt Arty and I get why she's angry."

I really did understand. I hadn't cheated on Arty in the way that she thought, and certainly not with Ollie, but I had known it was over a while before I told him. I had known I had feelings for someone else. I had tried to ignore them, but I couldn't make them go away and I knew I didn't feel the same about Arty. Those feelings were way stronger than anything I had ever felt for Arty. I loved Arty and still did, but not in that way.

I knew what I had said had hurt him, but he showed me nothing but grace, kindness, and understanding. I hadn't felt like

I deserved any of it, so when Lanie had found out and kicked me out, I felt like I deserved it. When Ollie found all that out and saw how Lanie was talking about me online, he didn't understand and had told me he would never let anyone talk to me like that again. I hadn't thought anything of it at the time, but I guess he took it more seriously than I had. I loved his need to defend me, but he didn't understand. There was no defense for what I did, and I deserved Lanie's anger.

Lanie looked down at me, surprised, and then reading the resignation and guilt in my eyes, with smugness. She had gotten what she was looking for, and I hoped that meant she would go away. Unfortunately, Lanie always had to have the last word and couldn't help adding to Ollie, "That's right, home-wrecker. Listen to your-"

She didn't get any further before I saw red. Her addressing me like that was one thing, but her dragging Ollie into it, her speaking to Ollie like that when his only crime was being my friend, was too much. I leapt across Ollie at her. I needed to be standing. I couldn't take this sitting down. I needed her to move, and I needed to be eye to eye with her. She needed to be stopped. I collided with Sadie before making it to the end of the booth. I had forgotten she was here. If I could have felt anything except anger at the moment, I was sure I would have been embarrassed at Sadie seeing me act like this.

Sadie stayed solid, not letting me go any further. *Fine.* Probably for the best, if I was being honest. I didn't push her any further, but stared up at Lanie without flinching or shrinking back, even though every instinct told me to shy away from her.

Even had I been standing, Lanie had a good six inches over me, but now, with me still in the booth, it felt like she was towering over me. I was surprised I wasn't cowering back from her, but I knew I had to be brave and stand up to her. Not for myself, but for Ollie. I wouldn't let anyone talk to him like that.

Slowly, considering each word carefully, I said, "Listen, Morgana." I mentally clapped myself on the back for remembering to address her as Morgana instead of Lanie. I was angry, but I didn't want to disrespect her, no matter how badly she had disrespected me. "I don't care how you talk to me. I know I hurt you when I hurt Art-" I stopped for a moment before correcting myself. "Arthur, and you are too bullheaded to move past any sort of action you view as personal, but you *will* leave Oliver out of it. He didn't do a damn thing wrong except be there for me when no one else dared to. He is the only one that cares about me, so you will leave his damn name out of your mouth."

She looked startled, impressed, and angry all at the same time. Ollie's jaw was on the floor, and Sadie looked impressed. I was proud of myself. I had probably made things worse, but I stood up for Ollie and I couldn't bring myself to regret that. I defended his honor, and that was something I knew I could be proud of.

"Or what, Pendragon? You're sure talking a big game there. Ready to back it up?"

I couldn't believe her. Lanie knew better than anyone that I didn't shy away from a challenge. She couldn't have really expected to speak to him that way and have me let her get away with it.

I made my bed, and I was ready to lie in it, but that didn't mean I would go quietly. I still had some fight left in me. "Anytime, anywhere."

I was surprised when her eyes lit up and she smirked. Her expression should have alarmed me, but I was too far gone to care. I had given too far into my anger to be scared of her anymore.

"If there's one thing I actually like about you, it's how easy it is to rile you up." I huffed. She was one to talk. "It's cute you think you could handle me."

I couldn't believe her. I expected more yelling, more anger, not this, whatever this was. I didn't know how to respond. I just knew I was tired of it, so I spoke without thinking.

"Any. Time. Any. Where. I tried so fucking hard with you. I was fucking terrified to end things, terrified I would lose you. I wasn't your enemy until you made me be. You keep pushing and pushing and pushing. It's a wonder you haven't pushed Arthur away, too." I gulped. I hadn't meant to say it. I shouldn't have said it. It was a low blow, and I knew it.

"As if, Pendragon. No one and nothing could come between us." I was surprised at how tame her response was. She seemed smug, like she was content to be verbally sparing with me. I didn't understand for the life of me how she could be feeling content right now, how she could be enjoying this rift between us and the hurtful words we were exchanging. Contentment couldn't be further from what I was feeling.

"There was a time I thought that about us. I hate how wrong I was."

"That makes two of us. It sucks finding out your best friend's girlfriend was a no-good cheating whore."

I didn't have a response to that. Ollie turned to me, unsure whether I wanted him to step in. I wasn't sure either.

Before him or I could do anything, I heard Sadie say, "That's enough." I gulped. Lanie wasn't going to like that, but she kept going. "I know you don't know me, but my friends over there organized a nice get-to-know-each-other dinner for us all. I won't let anyone ruin that. I understand you and Gwen have issues-"

I glanced over and saw Morgana was going to interrupt and braced myself for the inevitable, and was shocked when Sadie didn't let her speak. "But I don't care about that. What I do care about is that everyone is able to eat their dinner in peace without crying or without murdering someone. You probably are quite a nice person usually, so I am asking you to go take a seat and back off of Gwen."

I was shocked but I couldn't have been more shocked than Lanie was. She seemed at a loss for words before saying unsurely, "Well, you certainly won't find me crying." She met my eyes, and I sucked in a breath at how piercing her eyes were. It had been so long that I had forgotten how mesmerizing they were, soft and smooth, the color of caramel whiskey. Her eyes softened a moment as I watched, before her gaze hardened and the spell was broken. "What? Can't fight your own battles, Pendragon?"

I didn't respond. I couldn't. I didn't know what to say, and was too shaken from the way she had stared at me. I felt Ollie move and felt him take in a breath, ready to defend me. Without thinking, I elbowed him in the gut, harder than I meant to, since I heard an offended 'humph' from him. I couldn't bring myself to regret it, though. I needed him to stop. I couldn't take any more of this, and Sadie, miraculously, seemed to be succeeding at getting Lanie to calm down and leave our table. I couldn't have him saying anything that would rile her back up.

Sadie took control again. "Morgana, I think that's what you go by? If you have something else you'd prefer to be called, you can tell me and I'll use that, but for now, do you want to take a walk with me or go back to your seat?"

Lanie looked at her appraisingly. "And who are you?"

I expected Sadie to take offense to how she had said it. Most people would have, but Sadie didn't miss a beat. "I'm Sadie Hawthorne. Under other circumstances, I'm sure it would be lovely to meet you. Why don't you introduce me to your friends over there?"

I sunk back into Ollie's arms, relieved that this was almost over. I watched Lanie roll her eyes and didn't miss the look of disgust she shot me, but she didn't say anything else to me. "Fine, but don't think this means you won or that we're friends or anything like that."

I was shocked at how rude Lanie was being to Sadie, who was a stranger to us both, but the more I thought about it, the more it made sense. Lanie didn't know that I was only just now meeting Sadie. Lanie probably thought she was a good friend of mine, and Lanie would have been pissed that anyone dared to take my side.

I expected Sadie to be offended by that, but she didn't miss a beat before saying, "Of course not, but I'd love to meet your actual friends."

With that, Sadie solidified herself as one of my favorite people as she steered Lanie away from me. Even Ollie was impressed; I didn't miss the grateful look he gave her. I gripped his hand in mine and squeezed. The worst was over and we had survived.

It wasn't until Courtney cleared her throat that I remembered we had an audience.

Chapter Sixteen

Lanie

I couldn't sort through my feelings, and was still feeling whiplash as the girl—Sadie, I think—led me away from Gwen. I had been thinking non-stop about what our first encounter would be like, but I hadn't imagined it to go like that.

I had expected worse. I had expected anger from her and fireworks, the battle of the century, but I hadn't gotten that. She hadn't given me much of anything. She had actually looked like she had been about to cry when I came over. Part of me loved seeing that. That part of me was happy to see her unhappy, happy she knew how much she messed up, but it didn't make it any less surprising.

She hadn't even defended herself. I hadn't expected her to let me berate her like that in public without her fighting back. I had been thinking maybe she had lost her fighting spirit. Either that or she was playing up the sympathy of those around her. That must have been it. She was trying to make me look crazy by acting sane and apologetic, trying to make it look like I was overreacting and bullying her. That had to be it, because I couldn't face the alternative that she was actually almost in tears and I couldn't help but push her lower. I wasn't that type of person. Sure, I was angry, but that wasn't me. She had to be manipulating me and everyone around her like she was so good at doing. Like she had done to Arty and to me.

I had to break her, but it was easier than I expected. I was pissed at how easy it was that all I had to do was insult Lancelot and she cracked. She took everything I threw at her, but god forbid I insult her precious Lancelot and she flew off the handle.

I was thrilled I got her to break, but hated that it was about him, hated seeing how much she cared about him, hated seeing that she clearly didn't regret throwing away Arty, throwing away me, for him.

Sparring with her stoked the fire in me. I didn't care how she was thinking about me, as long as she was thinking about me. I hoped she lost sleep thinking of me, of what she did to him.

I took my seat and saw Sam, Eli, Ben, and Jade all staring at me, waiting for an explanation. It wasn't until I heard her voice again that I remembered I was supposed to be introducing Sadie to the group. Thankfully for me, she didn't seem too offended to have to do it herself.

"Hi, guys. I'm Sadie Hawthorne. I'm an attending author this weekend and I just wanted to say hi."

Crap, I thought, gulping. I had managed to offend one of the authors at the event. I had thought she was a friend of Gwen's from San Francisco, but it seemed highly unlikely now that that was the case. They might have just met tonight, and with how I was acting, of course Sadie would have taken Gwen's side. I would be surprised if everyone at Gwen's table didn't take her side after that.

I would have to be more careful and try to keep a leash on my temper. If Gwen's game was to make me seem irrational and mean, she was certainly succeeding, and I couldn't have that.

I really didn't want anyone thinking I was picking on her. I didn't want to be the bad guy or even look like the bad guy, but it killed me seeing her with him. Seeing her sitting on his lap, wrapped up in him, flaunting her happiness. I didn't know if she had seen me and was putting on a show, but it didn't matter. I didn't know what would have been worse; if she had noticed me and was doing it to piss me off, or if she had been too wrapped up in him to notice me at all.

Thinking about it for more than a second, I knew I was lying to myself. Her not noticing me at all was the far worse alternative. I had to believe she was doing it to piss me off. At least if that were true, she was still thinking about me as much as I was her.

I hated myself for it, but I missed her.

I risked a glance over at Gwen and saw she was smiling at him. I felt bile rise up in my throat when I saw she was still practically in his lap and holding his hand. Disgusting.

I turned away quickly, not wanting to see anymore. I heard Ben, Sam, and Jade introduce themselves. They were all gaping at Sadie and at me, waiting for an explanation, waiting to find out what happened. Sam discreetly slipped out their phone, frowned at it, and slipped it back in their pocket.

I heard Eli say, "I'm Eli. Great to meet you. Why don't you introduce me to your friends?"

I was surprised, but I shouldn't have been. Eli probably wanted to get her away from me before I could cause more of a scene. I was sure he would lecture me about it later. I knew Sam wanted the tea, Jade hadn't known us long enough to understand, and Ben was indifferent, but Eli would be pissed. Eli knew as well as I did how Arty would have felt about how I acted.

I hated that even now, Pendragon was getting between me and Arty, hated that I felt guilty for saying nothing but the truth to her, hated how she still got under my skin.

"Of course!" Sadie replied to Eli. "I'd love to. Come on over!"

I didn't miss the glare Eli shot at me when he rose, telling me to stay quiet. He didn't have to worry; I was embarrassed enough about my behavior that I didn't have anything else to add.

Chapter Seventeen

The second Eli was out of hearing range, Sam leaned closer to me. "Dude! What happened?"

I shot them a look that said I didn't want to talk about it, but even as I was doing it, I knew it wouldn't work. This was Sam we were talking about. There was nothing they loved more than some good, entertaining gossip. Sam's biggest complaint about our friends was how boring we all were. They would always say they really needed to make some more problematic friends so exciting things would actually happen. So I knew it was killing them to not have all the details immediately. I was honestly surprised they stayed in their seat at all.

If Pendragon had had a fan club in our group, Sam would've been its leader. They talked almost incessantly about reality shows together and about *TikTok* stars. Sam loved that

Pendragon always seemed to have some insider info about what was going on with a lot of the people we all followed.

I wondered if Sam still talked to her. I hoped not, but I hadn't had the nerve to ask. I didn't want to hear the truth if they weren't loyal to Arty and me. Well, really just to me, since Arty still talked to her. A fact which solidified why he always was and always would be too good for her. Despite me telling him numerous times to leave her alone, he never did. He was always checking in on her and making sure she was doing okay and seeing how things in her life were going. I'd even heard him ask her about Lancelot, though, of course, Arty used his actual name.

It was the only thing Arty and I didn't share, the only thing that we didn't see eye to eye on. I blamed her for that. Ever since she wormed her way between us, making our dynamic duo a threesome, we had had problems. Arty and I shared everything before her. Now there was a part of him that he didn't share with me, things that he felt he had to keep hidden from me. I hated knowing he felt that way, but when it came to her, I couldn't keep my temper and he knew that.

Sam was bouncing their foot up and down impatiently, staring at me.

"It went about as well as I thought. Had to make sure she was still a manipulative, lying whore. Don't worry, she still is."

Ben piped up, "Hey, watch the language. You shouldn't say that about anyone."

I was a little surprised Ben was standing up for her. I wasn't used to him contradicting me. Sam, definitely, Eli, all the time, but for Ben, it was unusual. I was confused until it occurred to me a moment later that we weren't alone. He probably thought I was being rude in front of Jade. He wasn't wrong.

I sighed. "Fine. I saw her grinding up on Lancelot over there and figured I'd tell her to stop giving us all a free show."

"You didn't!" Sam exclaimed, their eyes lighting up. They were practically bouncing out of their chair.

I was sure this was the most exciting thing they thought I had ever done. I was glad someone at least was happy with how that went, because I knew I wasn't. I had expected to feel better about things, to have felt some vindication, but I just felt sick. Whether that was from my own actions or seeing her basically giving Lancelot a lap dance, I wasn't sure.

"Fine, fine, no, I didn't, but I should have. If she keeps it up, I might."

"Come on, Mor, knock it off," Ben said.

He rarely ever protested anything, so I tried again. "You know I won't. Even though someone really should. I saw her all cuddled up with Lancelot, looking so happy and cute that I wanted to puke. I couldn't stand it. I don't think she even noticed me. She was too wrapped up in *him*. I saw red, so I went over there to make my feelings her problem. Why should I be the only one upset? Why should I have to feel awful when she feels good about herself and her choices? Why should she get to have a fun weekend when it kills me to have to tolerate being near her?"

Jade looked concerned, and Ben was watching Eli's back. He was still talking to Sadie. Sam grinned. "Of course, your problems have to be everyone else's. Very on brand for you."

They laughed, and I chucked my napkin at them, which they caught easily. Jade was watching us go back and forth, and Ben was on his phone.

"Well, she deserved it, but I expected a fight and didn't really get one. It was weird. She barely said much."

Sam looked skeptical. "It looked pretty heated from here, right?" They looked at Jade to back them up.

Jade looked embarrassed at being dragged into it, but added, "We saw her lunge at you. It looked a little heated."

"She *tried*, but Lancelot and that girl Sadie stopped her. Speaking of Sadie, pretty sure she hates me. I may or may not have thought she was a friend of Pendragon's, so I might've been a bit rude."

Sam seemed to consider a moment, saying, "Pretty close to your default, though. I bet she wouldn't have been able to tell the difference." I glared at them, but when they started laughing, I couldn't help the laugh that escaped my lips.

"You're no Princess Charming either." They laughed harder, and Jade smiled. I was glad the tension was over, but a moment later, I heard Eli over my shoulder. He pulled his chair out and paused long enough to sit before laying into me.

"What the hell was that?"

"Nothing more than she deserved."

Eli glared at me. "What you do or don't think she deserves is irrelevant. What does matter is that you know Arty would be hurt right now if he knew how you treated her, if he knew you treated anyone like that, really."

He was right, and I hated that. I wasn't about to admit that I knew he was right, though. Arty was *my* best friend, not his. Well, I suppose Arty was best friends with all of us, but it had always been him and I. Eli, Sam, and Ben were more recent friends. It was starting to piss me off that Eli was defending Arty from me, of all people, as if I would ever hurt Arty. Well, I amended, as if I would ever hurt Arty about anything except Pendragon.

I crossed my arms, not willing to give in. "You weren't even over there. How do you know I said anything? Maybe she pulled the first punch."

He continued to glare at me. "How do I know? Anyone with eyes would know you started that fight. You went charging over to her, and whatever you said made her mad enough that she literally lunged at you. Gwen isn't like that, so I know whatever you said had to be bad."

I shrugged. "Or she's just crazy."

Ben interjected with a cough. It was all that was needed to remind me Jade was here, and being rude to Eli in front of his cousin wasn't going to do me any favors. "Fine, I may have said a few things to her, but really nothing that bad. She lunged at me when I insulted her precious Lancelot."

Eli softened at that, and Ben piped up again, "He has a name, you know, and I know you know it since you've definitely checked out his socials."

I kicked him under the table, but the damage was done. Sam was bouncing up and down in delight.

I knew I would hear a lot about that later. Sam grinned wider, and just said, "Interesting," but I could see the delight in their eyes and knew this wouldn't be the last I heard of that.

Eli looked surprised, but recovered a moment later. "He has a name. It just isn't worth repeating."

I looked up, confused by his tone and words, but his face gave away nothing. I looked at Sam. Whenever you needed to know anything about anyone, Sam was your best bet. Our spat was instantly forgotten now that they were my best bet for uncovering the new mystery of what was going on with Eli. *He was just lecturing me about being kind to others, and now even he doesn't like Lancelot? There has to be more to the story* Especially since I knew Eli didn't mind Pendragon, so what was his deal with Lancelot? Sam looked intrigued, but shrugged. They didn't know any more than I did. Interesting. I would have to see what I could find out later, but for now, it was a good angle to use.

"I couldn't help it, man. You saw how all over each other they were."

He sighed. "It was too much." He paused for a moment before adding, "But you really shouldn't have. You're better than that."

I had to disagree with him on that, but I was happy he thought so.

"I'm sorry, man. I really tried but I swear they were doing it to get under my skin." Whether or not that was true, unfortunately, it had worked and worked well.

"I get that, but still. We have to be better than they are. We're not supposed to stoop to their level."

I wasn't sure what had gotten into Eli, but that didn't change the fact that he was right. We were better than that. I was a better person than her, and it was time I started acting like it.

Chapter Eighteen

Gwen

The second Lanie stomped off with Sadie, I felt the table's eyes on me. I kept looking down at my hands, hoping they wouldn't ask, but I heard a voice ask, "Are you okay?"

I winced, and felt Ollie do the same. I hated that question. It always made me emotional having other people ask me that. It pulled the emotion out of me against my will when other people cared enough to genuinely ask me how I was doing.

I looked up, cautiously, willing myself not to show weakness, not to cry. It was Skye who had asked. She brushed a few strands of her blue hair out of her face as she looked at me.

"That was really awful of her," Courtney said when I didn't say anything.

I shrugged. "It's a long story."

"You don't have to tell us anything," Skye rushed to say.

Courtney nodded immediately. "Seriously, we just wanted you to know we're on your side."

"And that we hope you're okay," Erin said.

"And that we're here if you want to talk," Skye added.

I squeezed Ollie's hand and said, "Thank you all. I'm really sorry that my drama got brought into our dinner, but I really appreciate you all being so kind to me."

"Are you kidding? Of course!" Skye said.

"Besides, you didn't do anything wrong. You were just sitting here minding your own business," Courtney added.

Erin nodded in agreement.

I thanked them again, and they seemed to understand I didn't want to be the center of attention and changed the subject. I was grateful for that.

To me, Ollie said quietly, "See? Perfectly reasonable, friendly people. Why you were ever friends with *her*, I don't understand."

I rolled my eyes, but he wasn't wrong. I had been worried about their reactions for no reason. They all had the kindness to give me space and not ask questions and I was incredibly thankful for that.

I felt my phone buzz again and pulled it out of my pocket, and almost dropped it when I saw who it was from. Sam. I gulped. Them and I hadn't talked since I left and as much as I had wanted to go say hi, I knew it was better to stay out of Lanie's way, and if I was being honest, I was worried about the reception I would receive from them and the others. I had been close with them all and had left without saying goodbye to them.

I hadn't just left Arty; I had left them all, and I didn't know how they felt about me being back, about me potentially being permanently back if I got my way with Ollie.

I took a breath and opened the message. **Hey there, gorgeous. Long time no see. Couldn't help but notice you from across the way.**

I looked up and saw their eyes on me and grinned. Some things never changed.

I quickly wrote back, **Like what you see, huh?**

I watched them tap furiously at their phone and then look up and shoot me a devilish grin. This should be good.

Definitely, they said with a winking face. **Purple hair usually isn't my thing, but he's pulling it off.**

I shot them a glare and saw them biting back laughter.

Another text came through. **Couldn't help myself. But seriously, G, I missed you. We all did.**

I couldn't help writing back, **Not all of you.**

I saw them roll their eyes, more tapping, and then I read, **Correction, all of us sane folks missed you. Sorry about Mor. She's a whole lot.**

I said the first thing that came to mind and hit send before I could change my mind. **Don't I know it. If you can sneak away at some point this weekend, I'd love to catch up.**

It was risky. I didn't want to ask them to pick between us. I shouldn't have even asked, but I meant what I said; I missed them. I hadn't realized how much until I was sitting this close to them without being able to talk. I missed Eli and Ben, too, and the old Lanie. Not this Morgana who hated my guts, but my Lanie. I knew she was in there somewhere, deep, deep down. At least I hoped she was.

I watched Sam glance up around his table and make eye contact with Lanie, who immediately looked over her shoulder. I quickly averted my eyes to look at Ollie, who raised an eyebrow at me. I pulled him in closer. He looked in Lanie's direction and from the way he glared at her and tightened his hold on me, I knew she was still looking at me.

I felt my phone go off again and looked down. **I'll try. I'd love to catch up, too. Talk soon. Xoxo**

I wasn't a yes, but wasn't a no either. I could be happy with that. I texted back a heart and put my phone away, satisfied.

The rest of the night was much less eventful, although Naomi did end up finding her way to one of the two hotel bars without telling anyone where she was going. Everyone at the other table, and Skye and Erin from ours, went looking for her. None of my old friends moved. Thankfully, Courtney stayed behind with me and Ollie and kept talking to me about cosplaying and books, keeping me distracted. She and the others were becoming fast friends of mine.

I liked them enough that I let Ollie drag me to the bar with them afterward. A few drinks and games of pool later, I was practically falling asleep on my feet. Only then did Ollie finally agree it was time to turn in for the night. I was grateful he let me doze off on the cab ride back to the hotel, only waking me long enough to get me upstairs and tucked into our bed before scooting in with me.

Chapter Nineteen

Lanie

Today was going to be a good day. I was going to make it a good day if it killed me. She had caught me off guard yesterday, but today would be different. Today I knew to expect her, and today I wouldn't let her get under my skin.

At least, that was the plan.

I didn't have to interact with her. I would hold my tongue and avoid her if it killed me. I couldn't have another outburst like yesterday, and I wouldn't, as long as she stayed out of my way.

I wanted to stop thinking about her, but as I sat there polishing my armor, I couldn't help my mind from wandering. I hated that thoughts of her still plagued me, hated that I couldn't stop picturing her smug smile and fiery hair. I hated that a tiny, miniscule part of me missed her, but I knew that wasn't real. I didn't miss her, not really. I missed the girl I thought she was, and that girl never existed. That girl wouldn't have ever hurt Arty how she did.

I slipped into the armor piece by piece and still couldn't shake her from my thoughts.

I heard a knock at the door and looked at the clock, surprised to find it was almost time to go.

I opened the door for Eli and did a double take at his silver hair. It had to be a wig, but it looked so real. If I hadn't known Eli was coming, I don't know that I would have known him. He looked the part, but I still questioned the casting. I thought for sure Eli would've been Dash and Sam would've been Felix. Sam was more naturally flirtatious and shared Felix's love of gossip. Eli was more subdued, but I knew when he committed to a cosplay, he fully committed, so this was going to be interesting. I just hoped he was waiting until we arrived at the venue to start.

"Before you say shit, just know if you start throwing yourself at me, Felix style, I'm not responsible for my actions."

Eli laughed. "I would never. I value my manhood too much for that, cupcake."

I stared him down for a few seconds before breaking into laughter.

"I'm surprised Sam didn't fight you to be Felix."

"Are you kidding? He fought me *not* to be. I was happy to be Dash, much more my style, but he insisted he was dashing like Dash and was 'not side character material'. He rolled his eyes when I laughed. So I'm our Felix. I was thrilled once Jade volunteered to be Ainsley, though. It would've been really creepy hitting on my cousin."

I shuddered at the thought for a moment before raising my eyebrows at him suggestively. "Maybe I should've been Dash then."

He rolled his eyes at me and groaned. "Not you, too."

I laughed. "No, not me. She is pretty, though."

It hit me a moment later that he seemed to be implying someone else was crushing on Jade. I was curious who, but he didn't leave me time to ask.

"Thank goodness, but yeah, you had your chance to join our cosplay." He looked me up and down before saying, "Bad ass armor, but are you sure about this?"

I knew what he meant, but I was sure. I wasn't changing my mind or letting her change my plans.

"Yes. I'm Cassandra through and through, and I'll be damned if I let her get in the way. There's no way I'm not wearing my armor. I worked so hard on it. Besides, she knows I'm here. There's a zero percent chance she comes as Ivy."

At least I hoped she wouldn't. She was bold, but she wasn't that bold. That would make a statement that neither of us wanted to deal with. If she knew what was good for her, she would steer clear of looking like Ivy and would steer clear of me. I knew I would be giving her a wide berth.

Today was going to be a good day. Maybe I would even meet another Ivy there, one worthy of the cosplay.

I let myself daydream for a moment about a mysterious redhead, but the vision soured when I noticed she had Gwen's face.

I banished the thought the moment it appeared. *No. Not today. Today is my day, and it is going to be perfect.*

Chapter Twenty

So far, so good. Either she wasn't here or she had been staying out of my way. Either way, I was happy.

Sure it would've been better if people had recognized my cosplay, but as much as it pissed me off to admit, it wasn't as recognizable without Ivy by my side. Just another thing she ruined for me. I'd have to add it to the very long list.

Even worse, the guys kept smirking at me when people asked who I was. They had all tried to talk me out of the outfit when Pendragon didn't drop out, but I was stubborn. I had thought she was smarter than that and would have dropped out. I had underestimated her, or overestimated her intelligence, because she was here.

Well, not *here,* at least not that I had seen, not yet. She would make an appearance, though. I knew she would. She would have to. She got her ticket for free to be at the events. She would have to be here. Odds were, she would come sweeping in any minute, dressed to the nines as Queen Guinevere, and people would swoon and bow at her feet. Disgusting. I hated that these people worshipped her, but I could deal with it. I didn't care what she came in wearing, as long as it wasn't Ivy's dress. If I were a better person, I would give her more grace. I knew she had worked on the dress for hours, perfecting it, but I couldn't bring myself to care.

It was my right to wear the armor, my right to cosplay Cassandra the righteous. I adhered to the knight's code and was worthy.

She wasn't even worthy to *serve* Ivy, never mind be her.

Yes, she was stupid enough to come back to town, but she surely wouldn't be stupid enough to show up in that dress. The dress that we had worked on together.

She wouldn't, I was sure of it, so why did I keep finding myself watching the door, looking for her fiery hair?

As we walked around and looked at the different books, talked to authors and to other cosplayers, I couldn't tear my attention from the door for long. I was searching for her face in every corner of the crowd.

I didn't even get to enjoy meeting Agatha Toller, which would've been a dream come true, but I knew what most people didn't; she was Pendragon's great aunt. I greeted her and told her I was happy to meet her, but having to search her face and watch her every reaction to see if Pendragon had poisoned her against me soured the encounter.

Next to Agatha's booth, I was surprised to see a familiar face. The girl from dinner, Sadie, the one I thought was Pendragon's friend. I still felt guilty about that.

"Hi," I said sheepishly.

"Hey! Morgana, right?"

I nodded.

"Great to see you! Love the armor!"

I felt myself blushing. Not at the compliment, but at how kind she was being. I had treated her terribly for no reason. If I were her, I wouldn't be being nice to me.

"Thank you," I said, "and about last night, I'm sorry-" I started, but she waved her hand at me.

"Really, don't worry about it. I know you're not like that usually."

How could she possibly know that about me? She doesn't know me. I was glad she was giving me the benefit of the doubt, though.

She must have read the skepticism on my face because she added, "I know you don't know me and I don't know you all that well, but you remind me of someone I care about."

"Who?" I asked, not able to help my curiosity.

I almost laughed when she gestured to her book. "One of my characters, actually. Inez. She's strong and fiercely loyal, kind, but has a stubborn side. You remind me a lot of her."

I couldn't decide if that was a genius marketing scheme or the truth. Either way, I had to applaud how perceptive she was. Even if she was only trying to dupe me into buying her book, after the way I treated her, I felt like I owed her.

I reached for the book, asking, "Tell me something. Does she get a happy ending?"

She tried to hide a grimace, but I had my answer.

I started to pull my hand back, but she added, "It's not an ending, so I don't know how to answer that. Things look bleak, but Inez is tough, and I'm still working on her ending. I won't make promises, but I will tell you, she's fighting like hell for a happy ending."

"Sounds like me," I said, chuckling.

"I really think you'll like her."

"Fine. I'm sold. I'll take it."

She grinned and rung me up, signing it with a flourish and throwing in a character art print of her main character Serena, and Inez. Looking at her, I knew Sadie was right; Inez was my type of person.

I paid her and thanked her before looking around for my friends. On instinct, I was looking for Eli, but couldn't find him anywhere. I caught myself looking for his dark curls before I remembered the silver wig. I still couldn't find him. I had a few false sightings over by Jordan A. Day's booth. There was a Felix chatting up a group of girls that were eating up the attention. From the giggling I could see, I knew *that Felix* was flirting hard, and probably wasn't Eli.

I went over to make sure, since I knew Eli was probably getting really into his role, but none of the six Felixes I saw over there were him.

Admitting defeat, I changed tactics and started looking around for Sam, Jade, and Ben. Knowing Sam, they were wherever the biggest crowd was. Even though they were Dash today, they would still want the attention, and it wasn't exactly out of character for Dash, either.

I heard cheers and followed the sound. When I got to the source of the noise, I couldn't help laughing when I saw what everyone was cheering for.

Sam as Dash and Eli as Felix were in the middle of a circle of people, sparing. While I knew how cool it would have looked with props, right now they didn't have any, so it looked like they were doing a weird interpretative dance. Jade as Ainsley was standing on the sidelines admiring them both with the rest of the people. I wondered for a moment if it was an act or if she was enjoying the view of Sam a little more than she let on, but I didn't know her well enough to decide.

I spotted Ben a moment later, standing with his back to the wall and one of his feet bent and braced against the wall. I met his eye, and he gestured to them and rolled his eyes. I grinned. I was sure there were better things we could have been doing with the rest of our time at the convention, but I knew if I tried to butt in, they would either drag it out longer or force me to join in. So I resigned myself to waiting.

Thankfully, they finished a few minutes later.

They announced Sam as Dash victorious, and Eli as Felix was pouting about how unfair that was. Only then was I able to pull them away from the crowd.

Ben came over and joined us. Sam and Eli high-fived and pulled Jade in between them, each linking their arms over her shoulder. I felt a pang of sadness at the sight and couldn't figure out why. Before I could think more about it, I stopped short, having almost ran into a woman who I hadn't noticed but, now that I had, seemed impossible to miss.

Standing in front of me was a gorgeous Amazonian looking woman who looked startlingly familiar. We had seen her outside earlier, but there was something more than that to the sense of deja vu I was feeling. She was dressed in dark brown leather that looked to be made for battle. She even still had her rapier strapped to her side. Good for her, although how she snuck a sword in was beyond me. I had wanted to bring a sword, but it was strictly against the weekend's no weapons policy, so I had left it at home. I sighed seeing hers. Without mine, my cosplay felt incomplete.

I knew I was staring at her and that I should have said something, but I struggled with what to say, still trying to place why I felt I knew her. I wasn't sure if it was the character she was cosplaying as or the person themselves, but something about her was familiar.

I was grateful when Sam spoke. "Great outfit! Who are you dressed as?"

She tilted her head and contemplated the question a moment before saying, "Surely I'm dressed as myself. Is it custom around here to dress as someone else?"

Geez, and I thought we were bad. She even had the nerve to look annoyed, as if we had asked her a stupid question.

Eli piped in, "So, who is yourself?"

She nodded, understanding now. "Of course, introductions. You'll have to excuse me. I'm new here. I'm Inez Cyneward of Sherbrooke, captain of the royal guard, at your service," she said, bowing with a flourish.

She looked up, and her gaze landed on me. She took in my outfit with admiration. "Nice armor. A fellow knight?"

I nodded.

"A pleasure," she said before glancing at a compass in her hand and then past us, "but if you'll excuse me, I'm on a mission that cannot be delayed."

She hurried around us, and we all exchanged looks. I couldn't help thinking that was a little rude. I watched her, curious about her destination, and saw she was heading to Sadie's table. That was when it hit me why I recognized her.

I grabbed my newly bought book and flipped to the character print I had put inside. Sure enough, the woman was a spitting image of Inez. She had nailed the cosplay. Sadie hadn't been exaggerating when she said I would like her. I would have to actually read her book soon. Maybe even come up with my own Inez cosplay if I liked the story enough, because I loved the look.

I turned back to the group and heard they were arguing about where to go next. I didn't really care, so I let them battle it out. I was looking around when I heard a tapping on my metal armor. I turned around and saw a young girl who was staring wide eyed up at me.

I smiled tentatively at her and asked, "How can I help you?"

She looked behind her at who I guessed was her mother. Her mother was nodding encouragingly. She turned back to me. "My mom says it's okay if I ask for your picture. I love your suit. It's so shiny!"

I grinned, and slowly knelt down on one knee, metal clanking as I did. "I'll tell you a trade secret." She leaned in closer, and I whispered to her, "I polished it myself this morning."

She giggled, and I noticed her mom was holding out her phone and recording. The girl called back to her mom, "Mom, I wanna be just like her when I grow up."

The grin on my face couldn't have been any wider, or my face would have split in two. Her mom took a few pictures, and I asked her to tag me if she posted it anywhere, handing her a card with my socials. She happily agreed, took her daughter's hand, and they kept moving.

I turned around to see a worried look on Eli's face.

"What?" I asked, worried already. "Did I mess something up? I thought she was happy enough. It seemed really cute."

He looked at me, confused, before shaking his head. "No, not that."

"Although you don't really need the ego boost," Sam chimed in.

"You're one to talk!" Ben added before I could.

Eli hadn't said anything, but I followed his gaze to the redhead he was looking at. I took a breath, but it felt like time had slowed down. She looked perfect, and I *hated* it. How dare she. She was wearing *the* dress. The one we had worked on together for her. Ivy's dress.

She had some nerve showing up in that. She must have wanted to turn heads. Well, if it was a scene she wanted, it was a scene she was going to get.

I took a step before hearing a hand clamp down on my shoulder. I looked back at Eli before shaking his hand off. This was one fight I wasn't going to back down from.

I stalked over to her across the convention floor and yelled out, "Pendragon!"

She turned slowly, and I watched as her skirt fluttered around her, peacefully. Too peacefully for how I was feeling, for the storm that was coming.

"How dare you?" I ground out through clenched teeth. The longer I stared at her, the angrier I got. She had no right looking that damn perfect, no right being here, dressed like that, like my other half. Cassandra's other half, I mentally corrected myself.

I glared at her, waiting for her to say something, anything.

She smirked at me and gave me a little wave. "Cassandra, there you are! I was waiting for you."

My jaw dropped. She couldn't have actually thought I would play along, did she? The crowd around us was staring back and forth between us, waiting to see who would make the next move.

I saw phones out, recording, and tried to come up with what to say, but I could feel the anger burning, feel my self-control dwindling. When I didn't say anything, she gestured at the dress and did a little twirl. I was mesmerized by the way the dress hugged her and the way the light danced on the beading. The beading that she and I had spent many painstaking hours doing together.

"You like?" she asked, smirking.

I saw red and felt the taste of blood in my mouth. Only then did I realize I had been both literally and figuratively biting my tongue.

"I'd like it better off of you," I ground out.

It wasn't until her cheeks flushed and the crowd "oooohh"ed that I realized how it sounded. My cheeks heated, and I stuttered out.

"No, not like that. You wish, Pendragon."

She was still blushing and shying away from my gaze. It was pissing me off that she hadn't dropped the Ivy act.

Pendragon wasn't a blushing schoolgirl, and she certainly didn't blush at anything I said.

"Cut the shit, Pendragon. We both know you're no Ivy."

She frowned for a moment, before saying, "I might not be as pretty as she is, but I feel like I look okay."

The crowd "awwwwww"ed and a few voices assured her she did. I glared at her and she just smirked back. Of course she looked phenomenal. That wasn't the point. I hated how easily she was twisting my words.

"Your looks aren't the problem. It's your ugly personality."

The crowd gasped, and I was satisfied to see the smirk wiped off her face.

I felt a hand on my shoulder and whipped around. Seeing it was Eli, I relaxed. "That's enough, Mor," Eli said quietly.

I shook my head. It wasn't. It wasn't even nearly close to enough for how much pain she had caused Arty and me, how much she had hurt us, and the damage she had done to his political career, and now she had the nerve to waltz back into *my* city, *our* city, and act like she was some sort of saint.

"No. It's not," I said to him, before getting louder and turning back to her, "I'm sick of the good girl act. Drop the fucking act, Pendragon. No one buys it for a second."

Ben stepped up next to me and tried to get me to move back, but I refused to budge. He looked at me with exasperation. "Come on, man. What's the goal? You said your piece. You got what you wanted."

"Got what I wanted?" I yelled. "What I wanted was for that piece of cheating trash to not be here. What I wanted was to not have to look at her face again. Clearly, I didn't get what I wanted. She's the one over here happy and smiling, so I guess I'll have to settle for wiping the smile off her face."

I turned back to her, and was startled to see her nearly in tears. I felt a pang of guilt for a moment before I remembered how good of an actress she was.

"Knock it off. No one buys the phony tears. It's hilarious you ever thought you could be Ivy. You're too much of a soulless, spineless, brainless, useless waste of a human being. You're the last person who should be wearing her dress. The dress we worked so hard on together." Thinking about the dress and the hard work I had sunk into it pissed me off even more. "You know, it's not even your dress. You only did part of the work, so part of it is mine." Before Eli or Ben could stop me, I closed the gap between us and grabbed her sleeve, pulling hard. "And I want it back."

I watched in satisfaction as the sleeve pulled loose, and grinned at the panicked yelp that came off her lips. I noticed a moment too late that her sound wasn't because of the sleeve and the ruined dress, but because the front of her dress without the support of her sleeve had slipped down. She caught it in time to keep herself decent; I was thankful for that. I was frozen in shock with my hand holding the fabric that had been her sleeve. She looked at me with pain and betrayal in her eyes that I felt I should've been more able to enjoy, but didn't feel nearly as good as I had expected.

Before I could say or do anything, I was roughly shoved away from her. I followed the hands to their owner and saw it was *him*. Of course it was him. *Lancelot*. The fact that he let me get this far in general was surprising in and of itself. Some knight he was.

I rolled my eyes at him. "Don't worry. I was just going." I looked back and saw Eli had stiffened and was surprised to see he was glaring at Lancelot, too.

Sam stepped out from nowhere and said, "Come on, Mor, let's go."

I nodded, but I glanced over my shoulder and saw Lancelot had turned and was comforting her. The sight nauseated me and I couldn't help yelling one last jab. To him, I yelled, "Some knight you are. Tell your girl to find a character better suited to her personality. Clearly, she's no Ivy."

I whipped around and moved away from them, stopping a moment later when I heard from over my shoulder, "Well, you're perfectly suited for Cassandra." I was confused by the compliment, until she added slowly, but with more power in her voice than I expected, "Pre character arc."

The crowd "ooooohhhhh"ed at that. I felt the insult hit its mark. Hard. I was ready to let her have another piece of my mind, but Eli's hand clamped down on one shoulder, Ben's on my other. Eli glared at me, but I didn't move. Until a moment later, I felt myself being pushed.

I almost threw my elbow, until I heard Sam's voice in my ear, "Way to go, hothead. Always have to be the center of attention, huh?"

I glanced around, remembering the crowd, and felt a pang of shame and embarrassment that was magnified when I remembered people were recording. I gulped and resigned myself to letting them pull me away. I had done enough damage for one day.

Chapter Twenty-One

Gwen

I couldn't tear my eyes off her as my old friends rushed her away. I couldn't believe her; couldn't believe she really hated me enough to humiliate me like that.

I felt the tears streaming down my face as I clutched my dress to myself, but I still couldn't take my eyes off her back.

As I watched, Sam was pushing her from behind, and turned around. They met my eye and frowned, mouthing 'I'm so sorry'. Before I could give them any sort of reaction, they turned back to their task and then they all were gone and I was left alone with Ollie in the middle of a crowd of people still recording me with tears free-falling down my face.

I should have moved, I should have done something, but I couldn't bring myself to do anything.

The moment they faded from view, Ollie turned back to me, took off his cloak, and wrapped it around me. I was grateful for the small comfort. He held it in place with his hands on my shoulders and guided me away from the crowd.

People were giving their condolences and saying how horrible she was, but I was still too stunned to react.

I hate her. Okay, maybe I didn't hate her, but I hated what she had done, hated that she wanted me hurt, that she hated me that much. I hated this rift between us. I used to feel like it was my fault, but I had tried with her. I had tried to be kind and give her space. I had tried to ignore her. Clearly, that wasn't an option.

I had tried to take the high road, but she insisted on sinking to new lows and dragging me down with her. I was done being the bigger person. I was done being apologetic and letting her walk all over me. She thought I was a villain before? She wasn't ready for just how low I was willing to go.

The next time I saw her, I would be ready and she wouldn't know what hit her.

Chapter Twenty-Two

Lanie

When my phone lit up way too early the next morning, I groaned and turned away from it.

I almost didn't bother checking it. I had slept terribly. Every time I closed my eyes, I saw the tears on Pendragon's face. Real tears. She was a good actress, but even she couldn't fake the surprise and pain on her face. I couldn't get her face out of my mind.

It was ridiculous. I should have felt victorious. She was humiliated in public. It should have brought me joy, but I was just feeling empty.

My phone wouldn't stop buzzing. Whoever it was was being insistent.

I groaned again, rolling back over to the phone. "Fine. Fine. You win." I said out loud.

I looked at the screen and saw Arty's face and felt my heart drop. Well, I was wide awake now, but I wasn't even remotely ready for the conversation I was going to have to have with him. I was going to have to tell him that Pendragon came back to town and that I blatantly ignored his request to leave her alone.

I hated that he cared enough to try to protect her from me. She didn't deserve it and she didn't deserve him, but as much as I hated to admit it, I was feeling guilty. I knew he would hate what I did, and I was ashamed of myself.

I thought about not answering, but I knew he would probably just keep calling.

I propped myself up on my pillow and hit answer, thankful the room was still dark and would hide some of my face.

When I answered, the anger on his face startled me I don't know that I had ever seen him look that angry in all the years I'd known him. There was no denying it. He knew.

"Who told you?" I was sure it was Eli. Although the more I thought about it, it could have been Ben, or maybe even Sam, because they would be loving the drama.

I braced myself, flinching away from the phone, away from the anger in his eyes. His voice came out quiet. I had to strain myself to hear it. "No one had to. Do you want to guess exactly how many times I was tagged in that damned video?"

Video. What video? I wracked my brain trying to figure out what he could be talking about before I remembered how many people had been filming our fight yesterday.

I gulped. "How much did you see?"

"Enough. I asked you to do one thing for me. One. How often do I ask you for favors? When was the last damned time I asked you to do something for me? It must've been a while ago cause I damn sure can't remember. I asked you to leave the poor girl alone. She's been having a tough time lately, and you literally ran her out of town. I asked you to leave her alone. What part of bullying her, ruining her dress, and trying to strip her in public was leaving her alone? What the fuck were you thinking?"

He never raised his voice, but he didn't have to. He almost never swore. Each swear word made me flinch, each one causing a pang in my heart. He was angry, furious.

"I know you're mad, and I'm sorry. I didn't mean to let you down, but you weren't there. You don't know what she did."

He glared at me, which shut me up real quick. "I don't care what she did. I don't care if she had her tongue down Oliver's throat in front of you. I asked you to stand down, to leave that poor girl alone, and you couldn't do that for me."

"I-"

"I don't really want to hear excuses. I tried calling her last night after I saw the video and she wouldn't even answer my call. You messed up, bad."

I sighed. "What can I do?" I could swallow my pride and apologize to her if I needed to. I didn't know how I would make it through that, but I knew in that moment that if Arty asked me to, I would. I was panicking. I hated that he was mad at me. He had never been this mad at me before. Annoyed, sure, but not actually mad. I needed to fix this *now*.

"Nothing."

He couldn't mean that. "Nothing?" I repeated, sure I heard him wrong.

"Nothing. You did enough and I don't know how to fix this now. She's going to leave, and I'm not even going to get a chance to see her again. I hoped she would stay until I got back at least, but there's not a chance in hell now. You made sure of that. I don't want you to do a damned thing except leave her alone. I don't care what she does or who she does it with, okay? Just leave her alone."

I nodded wildly and hurried to say, "I will, I swear."

He just nodded absentmindedly as he ran his fingers through his hair.

"Arty, you know I'm sorry, right? I wasn't trying to hurt you."

He sighed. "I know you're sorry, but I'm not the one that's owed an apology."

I swallowed, my throat feeling tight as I pushed out the words, "I can apologize to her."

"No," he said immediately. "I don't want you near her. I love you, you know that, but right now I don't trust you, not with her."

It felt like a jab to my heart. Trust was everything to me, and he knew it. I had to find a way to fix this, but I knew there wasn't anything I could do in this moment. "I understand, and I deserve that. I am sorry, though."

"I know you are, but right now, sorry doesn't fix this. I love you, but I *need* you to listen to me this time and actually leave her alone."

"I will, I swear."

He nodded. "Good. Maybe that'll be enough. Hopefully. I'm going to go. I want to try her again now that it's a more normal time there."

I held my tongue. I didn't like the idea of him talking to her, comforting her, but I knew better than to say anything.

"We'll talk later," he said before clicking off.

I hadn't had time to say goodbye, even if I had tried. I had never been so at a loss for words with Arty. I hated that I had let her come between us, but I wouldn't let anything like that happen again. I would ignore her until she left and then Arty and I could go back to our lives as normal. With any luck, I could get by without running into her today, so I would only have to face her at the ball tomorrow and then maybe the farewell brunch. I could do that.

I hoped.

Chapter Twenty-Three

Gwen

When Ollie suggested we go out, I almost didn't go. After yesterday's disaster, I didn't want to be in the limelight. I wasn't ready to potentially face fans, or anyone, really, and I definitely didn't want to risk running into Lanie. I knew I had to do something to put her in her place. If I didn't, she would just keep coming after me. She wasn't going to stop until she had driven me back out of town, but I couldn't let her, not again. This was my home, too.

I had wanted to reason with her, but she was being a bully, and there was only one way to deal with bullies, but I didn't enjoy the thought of becoming the person she thought I was. I didn't want to hurt her in the slightest, but she kept hurting me and I couldn't take it anymore.

I would have to take a stand at the ball. The ball would be my battleground and I had to prepare for war. I planned to stay hidden until then, but Ollie had other ideas.

Apparently, he had given his number to Skye, and they had made plans for us all to go dancing. I didn't mind the girls. Naomi, Skye, Erin, and Courtney were all nice enough, and I had had a fun time at dinner with them until Lanie showed up, but I was nervous about being out in public again.

I didn't want to hide from my problems, but I was more than okay with hiding from Lanie for a little longer and I knew they must have questions. They witnessed us fighting at the restaurant, at least. I wasn't sure if they had witnessed what had happened at the convention. I hoped not, but I knew a lot of people had and people would comment on it and ask questions I wasn't ready to answer.

I had been lucky so far that everyone was being respectful and kind to me, but I worried they might start getting intrusive and I struggled with handling that.

I didn't want to go, but Ollie insisted and since he had all but agreed to move to Portland, I let him drag me out. Of course, he made me change and get ready first, but that turned out to be kind of fun.

He picked out a lavender suit jacket for himself that perfectly matched the dress he picked out for me. It was a beautiful lilac overlaid with a white lace and hugged my curves. It even had a slit running up my thigh that I loved, but today it felt like too much.

I had looked at him and asked, "Are you sure we won't be overdressed?"

He looked offended and raised his hand. "Scouts honor."

I rolled my eyes. "You weren't ever in the Scouts."

He had pouted and said, "But I could have been."

We had both laughed, and that was that.

Now I was in the dress, and we arrived at the club, and it was clear we were overdressed.

I surveyed the line and noticed most of the people in jeans and cute shirts and looked at Ollie pointedly.

"Oh, come on!" he said. "Rule one, if you want to feel good, you have to look good. You needed a pick me up."

He wasn't wrong.

"Besides," he continued, "like I always say…"

"Life is an occasion; dress for it," I said in unison with him.

He offered his arm, grinning at me. I took it and made to get in the back of the line. He looked at me skeptically, saying, "Honey, no. Tonight we're VIPs." With that, he led me to the front of the line and the bouncer took one look at us and let us through the rope.

I couldn't believe that worked.

Once inside, I started looking around for Skye's blue hair. I figured she would be the easiest to spot, but I was struggling.

Ollie was standing next to me looking when I felt hands go over my eyes. I tensed up and yelped. A moment later, a familiar voice whispered in my ear, "Guess who?"

Sam. I instantly relaxed in their arms and felt myself being whirled around.

"Surprise!" they called out, and I wrapped my arms around them.

They spun me around in their arms before gently placing me back on my feet. I turned to Ollie to start introductions, but was surprised when he was smiling at Sam.

Hesitantly, I said, "Ollie, this is Sam."

I paused at his grin. "We actually met."

Sam pulled Ollie in for a hug, too. *What? Was something going on between them? Why hadn't Ollie mentioned they met?*

"I didn't know you guys knew each other."

Ollie blushed. He actually blushed. Maybe he did have a thing for Sam. I was giddy at the thought; him and Sam would be so ridiculously cute together. Then again, I was team anyone who kept Ollie wanting to stay in Portland. I was still processing the fact that I was responsible for his latest heartbreak, but I knew I would do anything to make him happy again.

"We actually met yesterday."

Sam was clearly enjoying Ollie being tongue tied. "I'd say we did more than meet."

My eyebrows shot up, and Ollie rolled his eyes. I looked to Ollie for something, anything. Sam loved gossip too much to clue me in, even though I was clearly begging for tea.

"Not like that." He turned to me. "You really weren't kidding when you said they make anything sound as dramatic and dirty as possible."

Sam shrugged. "What can I say? It's a skill."

I giggled, and asked Ollie again, "So what happened?"

"Nothing really. We met at the convention, a truce of sorts. I wanted some answers, and they did, too. Nothing important. It wouldn't have even mattered except for the timing. I rushed back to you the moment I heard her, but I should've been there. I shouldn't have left you, even for a second, and I'm so sorry."

That explains where he had run off to, and I had thought it was weird that Sam hadn't been with the others.

I put my hand on Ollie's shoulder. "It's okay. You're always there for me. You put too much pressure on yourself. You couldn't have known."

"But I should have."

"I should have, too," Sam added. "I'm really sorry. I should've been there, too. I have no idea what the hell has gotten into her, but I hope you know I know you don't deserve it. We all do. All of us have been trying to talk her down, Arty, too, but nothing's worked."

"I know," I said sheepishly. "I talked to Arty this morning. He apologized a million times and said she would leave me alone, but it's hard to believe that. She knew how much that dress meant to me. We worked on it for hours together and she ruined it, in front of everyone. I understood where she was coming from before, but that crossed a line. I don't know what will happen the next time I see her."

"Nothing will," Sam said quickly. "We'll make sure she's on her best behavior."

"I'll believe that when I see it," Ollie said. I knew it sounded rude, but I couldn't help agreeing with him.

"I hope that's enough, but I don't think it will be. She crossed a line, and I'm sick of it. The ball's going to be interesting, at least."

Sam looked at me with interest. "As much as I'm dying to know what that means, don't tell me. Plausible deniability."

I laughed. "You turning down tea? I hope you didn't go changing on me?"

They wiggled their eyebrows at me. "Me? Mess with perfection? Never. But, seriously, I know she's way out of line, but I'd rather not see either of you hurt, so I'll try to keep her out of your hair. So when Ollie invited me out tonight, I couldn't not say yes."

I looked at Ollie, surprised. "You did this?"

He grinned. "I knew you missed your friends. Sam was the only one who seemed approachable enough to ask."

"That's me, approachable, unavoidable."

We both laughed.

A moment later, Sam pulled their phone from their pocket and looked down at it. The smile fell from their face. They looked up at Ollie with a frown.

"No," was all Ollie said.

"I didn't say anything. I swear I didn't."

"You were supposed to stay way longer."

I wasn't sure of the entire context, but it sounded like Sam was leaving, which sucked.

"But you just got here," I said, knowing it sounded childish, knowing I was pouting, but I couldn't help it. I had missed Sam so much and it wasn't fair they had to leave already.

"Actually, it's not that," they said.

I was relieved for a moment until I noticed they still looked guilty. "So, what's wrong?"

"We aren't gonna get to be alone."

"No," Ollie said, crossing his arms.

They couldn't mean what I thought they did. "Eli's coming?" I asked with optimism, but losing hope by the second.

Sam looked devastated, but added, "Not just Eli."

Ollie swore, and I couldn't help saying, "But that's not fair. I barely had a few minutes with you. Why can't she let me be happy for more than five seconds?"

Sam looked torn. "She doesn't know you're here. None of them do. They only knew I was going out tonight. I made it clear I wanted to be alone, but Eli seemed to think I was upset and that they should be worried. He recruited Mor and the gang to come with him and try to cheer me up."

As much as it sucked, I was happy that they were all still looking out for each other. It was absolutely what I would have done.

"Well, I guess we better find the others then," I said, turning to Ollie who frowned.

"Actually, I don't know if they're coming."

When I looked confused, he added, "I did invite them, but my entire plan for tonight was to get you to hang out with Sam."

Sam frowned deeper. "I'm so sorry, buttercup."

I knew they were, but that didn't make the night any easier. They pulled me in for a hug. "I'll find more time to see you, I promise. I missed you."

"Love you. It's okay," I told them, trying hard to keep up a brave face as they pulled away.

"I have to go, but I promise I'll see you soon, before you leave. You aren't leaving Portland again without saying goodbye to me."

I winced, waving to them as they went to the entrance. "Should we go home?" I asked Ollie.

"It's up to you. I'm sorry our night was ruined. I can't believe they couldn't keep her away for a single night. That's all I was asking for. It's ridiculous."

I couldn't help but agree, and I felt bad knowing how much trouble Ollie had gone to to make sure I got to spend time with Sam, only for Sam to have to run off the second they got here. It really wasn't fair.

"We could go home, but I don't think we should let her ruin our night."

He looked at me in surprise. "Definitely not, but you don't actually wanna stay here, do you?"

"Well, I could take the high road and avoid her..."

"But?"

"But I'm sick of being the mature one. I'm sick of running away from her and I'm sick of her pushing me around.

I get she was hurt, but I've done everything I can to apologize and she keeps attacking me and I'm sick of it."

He looked at me with surprised approval. "You're not wrong. She deserves to be messed with. I can't believe she actually ripped your dress."

That still hurt. That dress was the last thing I had of our friendship and it was like she knew it, too, like she needed to destroy it, and I hated that.

"So, if you aren't taking the high road, what's the plan?"

I grinned. "You trust me, right?"

"Of course."

"And would do anything for me?"

He looked a little suspicious, but nodded warily. "Of course."

I motioned for him to move closer. "Okay, good. Here's the plan."

Chapter Twenty-Four

When I saw Lanie out of the corner of my eye, I turned and waved to her. Innocent enough, but I knew it would piss her off. I thought she would come over to me, but was surprised when she just scowled and turned away. I looked past her and saw Eli; I waved to him, too. He gave me a distracted wave before turning back to Lanie, watching her closely.

I was glad she didn't seem to be out for blood tonight, and thought for a second about backing down, but I couldn't. If I backed down now, I didn't know if I would ever get the nerve again. She might have been playing nice, but I knew it wasn't going to last, especially not when we were both in the same cosplay contest, vying for the same crown. Before all this happened, we were going to enter as a couple. Now I could only assume she was still entering and was out for blood.

I knew shit was going to hit the fan again with her sooner rather than later and was hellbent on making sure it happened tonight, not tomorrow at the ball. I had been looking forward to the ball for so long; I wasn't willing to let her ruin it for me. Even if she managed to hold her tongue and temper tonight, I knew she wouldn't tomorrow. It was better to get it over with tonight.

"Are you ready?" I asked Ollie, taking his hand.

"As ever," he said, watching the others warily. "Are you sure this is a good idea?"

I was surprised by that. I would have thought he would've been thrilled I was standing up for myself.

"Are you having second thoughts? You don't have to do this if you don't want to. I can come up with another way."

He shook his head. "It's not that. I'd do anything for you, you know that. I'm just worried about you. Are you sure you're ready for the fallout?"

I wasn't sure, but I nodded anyway. "Definitely. Better to get it over with tonight. Best case, she'll talk to me and we'll hash things out. Worst case, she'll blow up at me again and that should be the end of it."

He squeezed my hand. "As long as you're sure."

"I am," I said, but I wasn't.

"Here goes nothing," I said, and dragged him out onto the dance floor.

I stopped us in the middle, a good fifty feet away from Lanie, but I knew she was watching me. I grinned at her before turning around and starting to grind on Ollie. We were trying as hard as we possibly could to make it look sexy, but it was hard to not laugh. It felt like dancing up on my brother. I didn't have a brother, but that was how I imagined it would feel. Awkward and weird.

He bent his head to my ear, really selling the rouse, and told me, "That was quick. She's coming."

I braced myself, really getting into dancing with Ollie, really selling it when I felt hands on my shoulder. I was surprised that she actually touched me. She whirled me around to face her. Not missing a beat, Ollie grabbed my hips and pulled me back into him. I almost jumped, but stopped myself in time. I worked to move my expression to enjoyment. I was supposed to be enjoying this. Grinding up on Ollie was supposed to be natural, but with my ass up against him, it was hard to keep a straight face. I hoped he was faking it better than I was. From the anger on Lanie's face, I assumed he was.

Lanie looked at us with disgust before asking loudly, "What the hell do you think you're doing?"

I did my best impression of being unbothered and enjoying myself before saying, "Having a good time. You should try it sometime." I couldn't help myself; I winked at her.

I had to stop myself from laughing at the shock in her eyes. She glared at me, at a loss for words. A few moments later, she retorted, "My idea of having a good time doesn't involve being a hoe."

I grinned. "You haven't seen anything yet." I leaned closer to her and whispered, "Enjoy the show." I couldn't stop myself from flicking her nose like I used to.

Then, following the plan, Ollie spun me back to him and kissed me. I pressed my lips against his hard, raking my hands through his hair, moaning loudly. I felt his hand on the back of my neck and leaned into him harder. This was the first and last time we were doing this, so we really needed to sell it.

A moment later, I felt his body start to respond to me. We both pulled away at the same time, faces flushed. I was relieved to see Lanie had already stormed off. Ollie grabbed my hand and pulled me toward the back of the club. We needed some privacy.

He whispered to me while we walked, "Geez, warn a guy next time."

"It was literally the plan. Not my fault I'm too hot for you to handle."

"Come on. That was so not the plan. You were into it."

I rolled my eyes. "You wish."

He grinned. "If I wanted you, I could have you."

I laughed. "In a heartbeat. You know I'm yours, but not like that, never like that."

He chuckled. "Glad we agree. I was worried I was gonna have to let you down easy," he said, steering me to the coatroom. Seeing it was empty, we ducked inside.

I looked around. "What are we doing here?"

He glanced down for a moment uncomfortably. "Well, someone got a little carried away and I need a minute."

I laughed, and he added, "The plan was a kiss. In what universe what that just a kiss?"

I gulped, taking a step toward him, worried. "I'm so sorry. I didn't mean to cross a line."

He waved me off. "Nah, you're good. I just wasn't expecting that. No wonder Lanie thought Arty was that heartbroken. It's really a shame you're not a guy."

"If you were a girl, you wouldn't be able to keep me away from you."

He mimed flipping his hair over his shoulder. "Don't I know it? I would be a stunning woman."

We both laughed.

After a few more moments, he took out his phone and checked it. He looked concerned for a moment. "It's Sam," he said, scanning the message. "They have something to tell me but apparently it can't be over text." He rolled his eyes.

"That tracks. If Sam has tea, they'll want to see your face when they spill it."

"I'm starting to see that." He glanced at the door, unsure. "I hate that I'm curious, but I really want to know what they have to say. Will you be okay here?"

I nodded quickly. "Absolutely, as long as you promise to recap what happens. I would come with you, but after our little show, I probably shouldn't risk running into Lanie again tonight."

He agreed and left quickly, saying he'd be back soon and then we could leave. I was more than happy with that, so I pulled out my phone and started scrolling through my *TikTok* notifications. I had over a hundred, so I was thinking that would keep me busy until Ollie came back when I heard someone clear their throat.

I looked up, surprised. "Back so soon?" I asked Ollie, but lost my voice when I saw it wasn't Ollie.

It was Lanie. I froze. Crap.

Lanie smirked at me. Interesting. I knew there was a chance she would come find me to hash things out, but I had put the odds at one to one thousand that she actually would. I really believed she would steer clear of me and this would be the end of it.

"Prince Charmless get bored of you already?"

I had to hand it to her. That was pretty clever. "I don't know what you mean," was all I could say.

"Hardly a kiss anyone should have walked away from, so tell me, did he realize you weren't worth the trouble?"

She stalked forward, moving to me, and I cursed myself for having stayed in the corner when she showed up. She had been blocking the only exit, and I literally let her back me into a corner.

It wasn't that I thought she would actually hurt me; I knew she wouldn't. I just didn't know what to expect, and that made me nervous.

"I've told you, there was nothing between me and him."

"Please, that kiss was hardly nothing," she said, moving closer.

"It didn't mean a thing to me."

"You mean it didn't mean anything to him," she challenged.

"That, too. It didn't mean anything to either of us. We're not together."

She smirked. "If that's true, then you just go around kissing everyone like that." She was right in front of me now and leaned her arm on the wall behind me. I tried to calm my racing heart, but I couldn't breathe, couldn't think straight. "Do you really expect me to believe you could fake that kind of passion?"

That did it. I raised an eyebrow at her, challengingly. "Believe it or not, I'm just *that* good." Without giving myself time to reconsider, I said, "Want me to prove it?"

I watched the shock come over her face and then disappear just as quickly. She looked down at my lips, trying to decide if I was serious. I had never been more serious about anything in my life.

She put her hand up to my face. Without thinking, I moved into her touch. She cupped my chin before tracing my bottom lip with her thumb. I barely suppressed a moan. She knew what she was doing.

"If I didn't know better, I would think you were enjoying this."

She pulled her hand back, and I already missed her touch.

"Well, what are you waiting for? Show me."

I was still dazed from her touch. "Show you what?"

"Show me how well you can fake it."

I took a breath. She couldn't be serious. She was leaving me dizzy from just her touch; I didn't know if I could survive her kiss, but I saw the look of triumph in her eyes, and knew I couldn't survive that either.

I laced my hand around to the back of her neck, dug my fingers into her hair, and pulled her mouth forcefully to mine. If she wanted a show, I was going to give her one.

Every thought left my head when I heard her gasp. I bit her lip and ran my tongue over it. I dug my fingers more forcefully in her hair, pulling her closer to me while my other hand wrapped around her waist. A small part of my mind registered that her arms were still at her sides, and maybe I should stop. I was getting carried away, but with her lips moving against mine, I couldn't bring myself to care.

I went to turn us, to push her against the wall, but she was faster. She moved her arms and pushed me back against the wall hard before I could move.

I gasped, and she raked her hand down my side. When she got to the slit in my dress, she traced my thigh. I pressed myself into her and let out a moan. A moment later, she pulled away. I already missed her lips on mine, but I untangled my hand from her hair and let her move away.

She smirked at me. "Point taken, but don't you think the moan was a bit much?"

I stared at her, surprised, before I remembered how we got to this point. If we were back to playing games, I could do that. "I've never had complaints before."

"Makes sense. Men are easier to please. Women are a bit more of a challenge, not that you would know."

Dangerous territory. I didn't know what to say. We had gotten so off track from where I wanted this to go that it was hard to remember why I had done this in the first place, but I had things I needed to tell her.

"Can we be real for a second?"

She didn't nod or shake her head, just watched me expectantly. "I miss you so much, and I'm sorry, Lan-" Her face darkened, and I corrected myself, "Morgana."

"Wait," she said, considering. "That sounds too weird, doesn't it?" I didn't agree or disagree, worried at what else she might say. "Just you, just the once, you can call me Lanie if you have to. I don't want to be Morgana to you."

I couldn't believe my ears, but rushed to keep going. "I missed you so much, Lanie. You have to believe me. I never wanted to leave-"

"So why did you?"

I blinked for a moment. "Because you told me to."

She blinked at me. "What? When?"

How could she not remember the single most awful night of my life?

"The night Arty and I broke up, you walked in on me talking to Ollie and told me to get out."

"*Lancelot,*" she sneered out the name.

I rolled my eyes. "That's not his name and you know it."

"If you can fully convince me he wasn't the reason you broke Arty's heart, then I'll bother to learn his name."

"I told you already, he wasn't."

"Well, either he's responsible or you are. Which is it, Pendragon?"

"You know that sounds ridiculous, right? It's not even my real last name."

"I'll call you whatever I like."

"Fine, and fine. It was *my* fault, but I'm not a cheater."

"I heard you. I heard you tell Lancelot that you loved him."

I sucked in a breath, frustrated. "Think about that for a minute. How many times have I told you that I love you?"

"Lately?" she asked.

"Of course not lately, but back then."

She looked sheepish and admitted, "A few."

"And what about Sam, and Eli, and even Ben? I've told Ben I love him and you never once thought I was sleeping with Ben."

"That's different."

"Why?"

"Because you left us. You left Arty and went running into that homewrecker's arms."

"For the last time, there was and is still nothing going on between me and Ollie. I left because you told me to. That night, you told me to get out."

She threw her hands up in frustration. "Yeah, get out, as in go get a hotel for the night, go stay with Sam, go crash on Eli's couch, get out so we can talk in the morning. I was pissed and knew if I stuck around, I'd say something I regretted. I was worried about Arty and worried about you. He wouldn't even tell me what happened between you two, just kept saying something stupid about how he made a vow he wouldn't break. I was coming to check on you and, yeah, I was pissed that you were admitting your love to another man, confiding in another man. I was your best friend, and you hadn't come looking for me. You broke Arty's heart, and you were already telling another man you loved him. I couldn't stand it. I left and crashed with Ben for the night with Arty. I thought I was going to come back with Arty. That's why I told you to leave. I was going to get him from Ben's and drag his ass home, but Arty didn't want to come back yet. We didn't come back until the next morning. Imagine how it felt to walk in and see all your stuff gone, your room empty of everything that made it yours."

I was falling apart. I felt like my heart was breaking all over again. I was struggling to breathe and said the only thing I could think to, "You told me to leave."

"Yeah, for the night, not forever! I thought we all needed a breather and then we could sit down and talk the next morning."

"I-" I stopped, not even really knowing what to say. "I had no idea," I finished weakly.

"Clearly. You didn't take any time at all settling in with him. You left Arty and broke his heart."

"Arty and I are fine. He and I talked things out a long time ago. If he's forgiven me, why can't you?" I finally asked what I had been thinking since that night.

She was quiet a moment before saying, "Because it wasn't only him you left that night. You left me, too. I trusted you, and you left me."

"You told me to leave. I thought you wanted me to."

"You should know better than anyone how good I am at pushing people away. I just never thought you would actually leave. I thought you and Arty were the two people I could never push away and I hate that you proved me wrong."

214

"I-" I started, but Ollie barged in saying, "I can't believe them. That damn Sam has some nerve." He stopped short when he saw me and Lanie and felt the tension.

Lanie turned and pushed past him, leaving when he stepped toward me.

"Lanie, wait!" I called out, but she didn't stop.

Ollie looked at me for a moment before pulling me into him, and then the tears came.

I couldn't believe it. I had had no idea how she was feeling, but I should have known better. I knew her, the real Lanie, not the one she showed the world. I should have known. I had to find some way to make it up to her, some way to fix things, if she would let me. I had to try, otherwise I didn't know if the hole in my chest would ever mend.

Chapter Twenty-Five

Lanie

There wasn't a chance in hell I was sleeping tonight after that.

I had to find Eli, or Sam, or even Ben and get the hell out of here. I didn't know where I wanted to go, but I couldn't stay here. I couldn't face her again yet. Not after what we just said, after what we just did.

I could still taste her lip gloss. She tasted of strawberries and honey. I could still feel her lips on mine. How she could kiss that well, get that into a kiss that meant nothing, was beyond me.

I couldn't fake it that well. That kiss was hot, and I'd die before admitting it, but I had gotten lost in her. I knew I was only caught up in the moment, but I couldn't remember the last time I had been kissed like that.

It felt like more than a casual kiss, but I would sooner die than tell her that. She was only trying to prove her point, and, damn, did she prove it. If she could kiss me like that without it meaning a damn thing, then maybe she was telling the truth about her and Lance ... Oliver, I corrected. It was possible they weren't together, possible they never were, but if that were true, it only left me with more questions. Why did she and Arty break up in the first place?

Arty. Shit, I needed to call him I couldn't believe it had taken me that long to realize I had just kissed his ex-girlfriend. Well, technically, she had kissed me, but it was the same thing. My lips weren't exactly innocent. I needed to call him immediately, but I needed to get out of here first.

Still heading to the door, I more frantically scanned the crowd for my friends. Almost instantly, I spotted Sam. They were dancing with someone I didn't recognize, and I thought about interrupting but decided against it. Sam would be living for the drama and would want to know every detail. I found Ben close by and considered, but it wasn't really Ben I wanted right now. I found Eli looking pissed while standing near the door and grabbed him.

"Woah, what's going on? What's the rush? Where's the fire?" he yelled as I dragged him outside. "What did you do, man? Crap, is Gwen okay? Tell me you didn't do something bad?"

I led him to his car. "Open it. We have to talk."

He clicked the doors unlocked, and I yanked open the passenger door of his Toyota Avalon and sat down, pulling the door shut hard behind me.

"Careful! Watch the car. She didn't do anything to you!"

"Sorry, Ava," I said, giving the door a light pat.

"That's better. She didn't mean it, Ava. So, spill. What's going on?"

"I will. We'll talk, but I have to call Arty first."

He looked at the clock. "Isn't it a little early for that?"

I did the mental calculations quickly. "It's probably 6am there now. He might be up, but it doesn't matter. I need to talk to him. It's an emergency."

Eli knew better than to think he could talk me out of it, so he didn't try.

I thought about doing a voice call with Arty. I wasn't sure I wanted him to see my face right now, but we always Facetimed. He would know something was up immediately if I didn't show him my face. Maybe if he saw my face, he would know how upset I was about this whole thing and would forgive me quicker. I tried to remind myself this was Arty; he was bound to forgive me quickly anyway, but I knew I had crossed a line. I just hoped it wasn't an unforgiveable line.

I clicked his contact and stared at my phone, clutching it hard, waiting for him to answer.

"Come on, man. Pick up."

"He might still be sleeping," Eli supplied.

"Not helpful. He's gotta wake up. I'll keep calling until he does."

Eli let out a breath. "Shit. That serious?"

"That serious."

I sighed in relief when a ring later, Arty's face showed up. I could tell he was still in bed and it looked like I had woken him up. I almost rolled my eyes at his golden hair still looking perfect, not a strand out of place, but this was serious.

"Lanie, everything okay? Everyone okay?"

He was kind enough to not mention how early it was there or that I had clearly woken him up.

"No. Not even remotely."

He sat up, alarmed, and gave me more of his attention. "What happened?"

"Short or long?" I asked, knowing the answer before he even responded.

"Short than long, obviously."

I winced. "I'd rather not give the long, and before I give the short, you have to know how sorry I am. I didn't mean for anything to happen, and I promise I would never try to hurt you."

Arty looked confused and worried, and I noticed Eli's expression mirrored his.

"Oh yeah," I added. "Eli's here, too."

I turned my camera quickly to him. "Hey, Arty," Eli said quickly. "We miss you, man."

"Good to see you! I'll be home in a week. Miss you all, too, though. Any idea what this is about?"

"None," Eli told him. "She wouldn't tell me."

I turned the camera back to me in time for Arty to say, "Whatever it is, spit it out. You're scaring me."

"I'm scared," I admitted. "I'm worried you're going to hate me."

He took a deep breath. "I know you're scared and worried, but you know me. We've known each other forever now. We're family. I might not love what you're going to tell me, and I might even be angry, but I'm not going to and never could hate you. We're family. I love you, you know that."

I gulped. I was the one that should have been pleading with him, not the other way around. He was being really nice to me now, but he didn't know what I did. I had to tell him. I was going to burst if I kept it in a moment later.

"Gwen and I kissed."

"WHAT?" Eli yelled so loudly he snapped my attention away from Arty. "WHEN, HOW, WHAT?"

I didn't know what to say to Eli, but his reaction was making me glad I hadn't brought Sam with me. If Eli was reacting this over the top, I couldn't even imagine how Sam would have reacted.

It wasn't until I heard him chuckle that I remembered I was supposed to be focused on Arty.

I turned back to the phone, sure I was hearing wrong, but he was laughing.

"What?" I asked.

"You're not messing with me, are you? That's really what happened?"

Crap. Of course he thought I was joking. He was going to be pissed when he figured out I wasn't.

I nodded slowly.

He grinned.

"You're not mad?"

"Mad? I was worried you two were going to kill each other, not kiss each other. What happened?"

"So, the short is that I dared her to make out with me in a coat closet."

Eli gasped. "YOU DID WHAT?"

Arty laughed again. "I agree. We're gonna need the long. I'm hoping the long makes more sense."

I let out a laugh, relieved. "I doubt it, but here goes."

I told them about everything that happened leading up to the kiss, and was about to get to the kiss when Eli interrupted me, "Wait, go back. She said her and Oliver aren't together?"

I had glossed over that because it wasn't even remotely the most important part of the story, but humoring him, I explained, "Yeah. If she was telling me the truth, they never were."

He looked stunned. "But you said you caught them in a compromising position."

"I did. I heard her tell him she loved him with my own ears."

Eli looked at me in shock before his eyes narrowed. "That was it? You made it sound like they were having video sex, and all she did was tell him she loved him?"

I didn't know what to say, but Eli kept going, "Man, do you know how many times that girl has told me she loves me? Do you think we're doing it, too? Actually, no, don't answer that. I don't want to hear it. I can't believe I believed you. I can't believe...I....I can't believe this."

I was left gawking at him when Eli opened the car door and stormed off.

I looked at Arty, stunned. "What just happened?"

He looked as confused as I was. "I have no idea what that was about, but you might want to go after him."

"I don't know. I think he might need some time to cool off. Besides, you and I aren't finished talking."

"I don't really need to hear the rest," Arty said.

"But I think you should. If you don't hear it all, I'm going to be worried that later you might and that something I did will make you mad at me."

He sighed. "It won't, but okay, if you need to tell me, then keep going."

I did. I told him everything about the kiss and about me leaving her.

That was the part he interrupted. "And you just left her? You guys didn't hash out what happened and what it means?"

"Of course not. We didn't have to. I know it didn't mean anything to her. She might not be with Lance—Oliver, but that doesn't change the fact that she's straight as an arrow."

He didn't say anything, didn't agree or disagree, but asked, "Ignoring how she feels for a second, did it mean anything to you? How do you feel?"

I groaned. "Geez, why are you always so nice and understanding? Yell at me, make me feel terrible for this, anything, come on."

"If you wanted a fight, you called the wrong person."

"I know, I know, but geez, I didn't expect to be sitting here talking to you about how it felt kissing your ex."

"You're not. You're sitting there trying to avoid talking about how it felt kissing my ex."

"I don't know, man. Does kissing ever not feel good?"

"Absolutely. Remember Donnie?"

I groaned. How could I forget the first and only time I ever kissed a boy? We were still kids, and he slobbered all over my face like a dog. If being gay were a choice, that would have been the day I made my choice.

"Fair point. She wasn't at all like Donnie."

He grinned. "So what you're saying is...."

He was really going to make me say it. "Fine, yes, what I'm saying is I enjoyed it. Happy?"

"For now. What I really want to know is how it made you feel."

"I would tell you if I knew, but I have no idea, and besides, it doesn't matter. In no world did it mean anything to her, so my feelings, whatever they end up being, don't matter."

He seemed like he wanted to say more, but for whatever reason, held his tongue.

"If you say so. Anyway, thank you for telling me. I still trust and love you, and am not even remotely mad at you. In fact, if you ever wanted to get with Gwen or any of my other exes for that matter…" I started to protest, but he kept going. "I know, I know, just hear me out. You have my full blessing, my irrevocable stamp of approval. I am one hundred and twenty percent behind anything that makes you happy."

"You're seriously ridiculous and too good to me, and that's completely unnecessary and out of the question."

"I just wanted you to know. You support me without question and I love you the same way, without question."

I smiled. "I'm glad we have each other. Now hurry up and get home so I don't have to parent the group on my own."

"Yes, dear," he said with a laugh. "Try not to kill anyone until then. I'll be home in a week."

"I know, I know. On my best behavior."

"Well, I'm going to go get a bit more sleep, but maybe go check on Eli and have fun at the ball tonight!"

With that, he clicked off, leaving me staring at the phone. It technically wasn't tonight for us yet. There were a couple more hours before it was the day of the ball, but with everything going on, I had forgotten about the ball, that I would have to face her there. That I would have to see those lips of hers that I had kissed, that I might even have to talk to her.

I didn't know how I would make it through, but that was a problem for tomorrow. Tonight I needed to find Eli, figure out what had gotten into him, and get the rest of the gang and get home, preferably without running into Gwen again.

I hopped out of the car and started back toward the club. I found Eli outside with Ben. Sam wasn't with them, though.

I rushed over. "Hey, Eli, about earlier, man-"

I was about to apologize, still not really sure why, but he waved it off. I looked at him and was relieved to see he didn't look angry. "No worries. I overreacted a bit. I was just surprised. We all trusted how you told the story, and I did and said some things I probably shouldn't have."

Ben piped in, "It wasn't your fault. I'm sure Gwen understands."

I looked at him questioningly. "Eli gave me the shorter than short version."

Eli added quickly, "That Gwen never cheated on Arty and that you and she had a heart to heart."

I nodded. I would fill him in later, and Sam, too, but right now I was more focused on Eli.

"She'll forgive you. She's the type," I told him.

He looked thoughtful. "Yeah… yeah, you might be right. Maybe he... Maybe Gwen will forgive me. I just have to talk to them, make things right somehow."

I nodded quickly. "Yeah, I'm sure that'll fix it, but I'm so sorry. If you need any help, let me know."

"No. I've got this. I messed up and I have to fix it. Besides, you did enough."

"I know. I'm sorry."

Eli looked at me for a long minute before saying, "I know you are. It's not your fault. I made my own decisions. They tried to explain and reason with me, but I was too stubborn to listen, but now that I know, I'm going to try to fix it."

I just nodded. I had no idea he had taken Gwen leaving so hard. He had hidden it well. I patted him on the back. "Well, anything you need, we have your back."

"Thanks guys. I just want to go home and get some sleep." I was relieved to hear him say that. I didn't know if I would get any sleep tonight, but I wanted to be home in my bed. "I just have to go grab Jade and we can leave."

With everything that happened, I had forgotten Jade had come with us. "What about Sam?" I asked.

"I'll see if they want to come, but they found their own ride here so they can get themselves back."

Sam didn't drive, but there was a good chance they weren't ready to leave yet, and if that were the case, they might stay until the place closed and get an Uber. If they weren't ready to go, there was no dragging them off the dance floor.

Eli came back a couple minutes later with a concerned looking Jade in tow, who was asking him questions he wasn't answering.

He looked out of it. That made two of us.

I hoped with rest that both of us would feel more in control and less confused tomorrow, but I doubted it.

Chapter Twenty-Six

Gwen

"You did what?" Ollie yelled in the middle of the coffee shop.

I hadn't told him about what happened with Lanie last night yet. He had seen me crying and assumed things went badly. He hadn't asked, and I hadn't told him differently until now.

"How could you keep that from me? And where the hell did that come from? I thought you hated her? I thought you were pissed at how she was treating you and what she was doing to you. What happened? I thought you were still getting over someone."

I didn't know where to start. Luckily, Aggie came in then.

"Saved by the Toll-er," I joked, getting up and hugging her.

When we both sat down, Ollie turned back to me. "Okay, spill. I need details, and I need them now."

I rolled my eyes. "You can wait. I don't have much longer with Aggie."

"I'm not that old, dear." She laughed.

"No, but you are..." I paused, looking back and forth for a moment, and leaning in closer to them both, whispering, "an east coaster."

She cackled. "The horror."

"I know you leave soon and I don't want to keep you long, but I needed to talk to you."

"I wouldn't dream of leaving without saying goodbye."

"I know. I know. But things got a little out of hand yesterday and I need your advice."

"Out of hand how? What happened? Are you okay? You didn't meet Damien, did you?"

Ollie and I exchanged a confused look before I asked her, "What? Who's Damien?"

"Never mind," she said, shaking her head, relieved. "So, what happened? Are you okay?"

"Mostly. It was an emotional night. Lanie and I finally talked about everything."

"And, apparently, did more than talk," Ollie added pointedly, making me blush.

"Wait. You guys got together?" Aggie asked.

I shook my head quickly. Not knowing what she counted as getting together and not wanting to ask. "We just kissed."

"Passionately, in a coat closet," Ollie added. I kicked him under the table before he could say anything else.

"Hey!" he exclaimed.

"She doesn't need the details."

"Au contraire. I absolutely do. How was it?"

I blushed, unsure what to say.

Ollie butted in before I could say anything and asked, "Was it better than ours?"

Aggie looked at us, shocked. "But I thought you two weren't...?" She pointed back and forth between us, not finishing her question.

"We're not," I said, glaring at him. I wanted to talk to Aggie about how I was feeling, but I hadn't planned on telling her *everything*, just enough so she would understand and could give me some advice. "But, yes, it was."

"You're just saying that to get me to shut up."

Yes and no. I wanted him to stop talking, but I wasn't lying.

"Wait," Aggie said, and I could almost see the dots connecting in her mind. "Is Lanie *the* girl?"

"What girl?" Ollie asked.

I nodded.

Aggie's eyes widened, and Ollie pouted. "Wait, no fair! What girl? What am I missing?"

Aggie looked at me with a sparkle in her eye and smiled. "Do you want to explain, or should I?"

I sighed dramatically. "But having him in the dark is so much more fun."

"Hey!"

I laughed. "Fine, fine. I might as well admit it. Lanie's the girl I fell in love with, the reason I broke up with Arty in the first place."

His eyes bulged out of his head, making him look like a cartoon character. "Lanie? You can't mean that. Morgana? After everything she's put you through?"

"She's a strong person, but she was really hurt when I left. I had no idea how badly. I thought she was only mad about Arty, but she told me last night that wasn't it. She was upset I left her, too."

"Didn't she tell you to leave?" he asked.

"She did, but apparently she just meant for the night. I didn't bother to ask."

"You couldn't possibly have known that, though," Ollie said.

"I know," I agreed. "I had no idea that I had hurt her, too. On the plus side, I think she finally understands that I wasn't cheating with you."

"So, what now?" Aggie asked. "Are you going to see her again?"

"I mean, she'll be at the ball."

Ollie huffed. "I don't think that's what she meant."

"It wasn't, but that gives me an idea." The twinkling in her eyes told me it was going to be a terrifying, but genius, idea. "Do you have any idea how she feels?"

"I don't. Even before this all, I never really knew. I didn't even know myself how I felt for a long while. When I figured it out, I was too worried to say or do anything. I was dating Arty, and I would never come in between them. When I ended things with him and told him, he gave me his blessing, but I never got to talk to her. I never even decided if I was going to. He told me he thought she felt the same, but he admitted they had never talked about it, so I don't know."

"I can't believe you never told me," Ollie said.

"After I left, her and I never even talked, so it stopped mattering. You didn't tell me about your boy, either."

He shrugged. "Fair point, I guess."

"So, are you ready to tell her? And if she feels the same, would you be ready to come out?" Aggie asked.

I thought about it for a minute. That was a big question, but it was something I had been thinking about for a long time. "I think, regardless of how she feels, that it's time. I'm sick of hiding."

Aggie broke into a grin. "That's my girl. Life's too short to stay hidden and love's too rare to not fight for."

Ollie looked at me for a long moment and asked, "Are you sure?"

I nodded. I had thought long and hard about when was the right time to come out, and had come to the long overdue conclusion that there was no right time. If I spent my life waiting for the right time, I would be left waiting forever. I could do this. Ollie would be there to support me. I wished Aggie could be, too, and Arty, but Ollie being there would have to be enough.

"I think I want to come clean about why Arty and I broke up, too. I want Lanie to know the truth. Even if she doesn't forgive me, even if she doesn't feel the same, I want her to know. I want her to know that loving her, falling for her, was worth everything and I'd do everything all over again if it led me back to her."

"Oooooof," Ollie said with a whistle. "You've got it bad, don't you?"

Aggie clapped her hands together. "How do you feel about grand gestures?"

I looked at Ollie, who raised his eyebrows, intrigued. Aggie was a writer, after all, so I knew this had to be good. I wasn't completely sure about it, but a ball seemed like the perfect place for a grand gesture.

"I have a plan," Aggie said.

When she was done giving me her suggestions, and Ollie and I had tweaked it a little to make it perfect, I pulled out my phone. I scrolled through my contacts looking for Kodie's name. She was the founder of the Ball and had been kind enough to invite me as an influencer. I considered her a friend of mine, and I was going to need her help to pull this off. I hoped she would be on board. I crossed my fingers and made the call.

Chapter Twenty-Seven

I was nervous, but it was too late to turn back now. Kodie had loved the idea and had made a few minor changes to fit it into her program for the night. I was surprised at how unphased and supportive she was when I explained what I was doing and why. I had expected more surprise, but if she was surprised, she hid it well.

She was instantly on board, and I didn't get the feeling it was for extra publicity, although I knew it would help bring attention to the ball, and I was more than happy to do so.

The more I thought about what I was planning to do, the more nervous I got. Ollie was going to live stream it for me, so I didn't have to do it more than once, but I was freaking out about all my followers finding out. I hoped they would all be kind about it, but realistically, I was expecting to lose some of them by coming out. It was unfortunate, but it seemed inevitable. I hoped most of them would be supportive.

I had held myself back for too long and didn't want to keep hiding. I was ready. I just hoped I was ready for the consequences.

I looked in the mirror again, making sure my hair was in place. I had tied part of my hair up and left some curls hanging down. A curled auburn strand that was pulled back had come loose. I went to tuck it back before reconsidering. It wasn't perfect, but neither was I, and I liked it that way. I took in my blue silk gown and was ecstatic about how amazing it looked. The lace cap sleeves were beautiful and delicate. When Lanie had suggested the fabric, I had known no other would do. The fabric was very much Ivy, but more importantly, it was me. She had said it matched my eyes, and it was startling to see how right she was. In this dress, dressed as Ivy, I had never felt stronger or more myself.

In another life, I had made this dress to win a cosplay contest with my best friend. Now I was wearing it against her, but I couldn't care less whether I won the contest. The contest was the furthest thing from my mind. I just hoped my plan worked. One way or another, tonight the world would know.

One way or another, I would know how she felt about me. There would be no hiding anymore, and while I was terrified, I could taste the freedom ahead and was itching to reach out and take it.

Chapter Twenty-Eight

Even my nerves couldn't stop me from marveling at the beauty and other-worldliness that greeted me when the doors to the ball opened.

When Kodie and I had talked, she insisted I come early to film some content and to see the place. I was grateful to have some time to enjoy the space before everyone else got here. Pretty soon I would be surrounded by other people and would have to start worrying about my plan, but not yet. Right now, it was only me and Ollie, right now I could take a minute to be at peace and enjoy myself.

Ollie held out his arm, and I looped mine through his and took a step in. We were engulfed in fog that was lit up purple. A few steps later, when the fog cleared a little, I gasped.

If my lashes weren't coated in mascara, I would have rubbed my eyes, sure I was seeing things.

Somehow, impossibly, in the middle of the lobby was a giant tree. I moved closer, putting out my hand, and gently ran my fingers over it. It was handcrafted. I didn't know what was more unbelievable, that it would have been real and in the middle of the lobby or that someone had made it. If I hadn't touched it, I would have thought without a doubt that it was real.

Ollie stepped back, and I saw him pull out his phone and start pointing it at me. Of course! I was supposed to be filming content. I didn't know what I would do without Ollie. I grinned at him and did a twirl. At the same moment, the fog machine spit out more fog, engulfing me and my dress in otherworldly beauty. As I spun, my blue ball gown flared out in waves. I was grateful Ollie caught the moment.

I looked at him questioningly, wondering if he would stop filming so we could keep going together, but he waved me on. I looked around the tree and noticed for the first time what looked like a stone drawbridge.

I audibly gasped and gathered my skirts and ran through the archway. It was a dream come true, out of a fairytale, and I couldn't wait another moment.

From somewhere behind me, I heard Ollie laugh and call out, "Gwen!"

I slowed, turning around and going back through the arch to see what he wanted.

"You're supposed to be better at this than I am. We need more than that. Wait for the fog to go again and then pop out from the archway and wave me in. I'll follow you this time. Just don't run."

"What, you can't keep up?"

"If every single one of my elementary, middle school, and high school gym teachers couldn't make me run, neither will you."

I laughed hard, ducking back behind the arch out of sight. A moment later, I heard the hiss of the fog and moved forward to meet him again.

Chapter Twenty-Nine

Lanie

I hated to admit it, but I was nervous. Confused, too, but mostly nervous. There hadn't been a single moment since I left the club that Gwen hadn't been on my mind. I didn't know what the hell to make of what happened, and I wasn't ready to face her yet.

I dragged my feet the whole way here, and while I had originally planned to get there right when the doors opened, we all ended up being a half hour late. Thankfully, it wasn't just me. Eli had been in a daze all day and Jade had to keep prompting him to get ready. Ben kept telling us loudly that if we took much longer, he wasn't going. Ben hated being late, but I couldn't bring myself to rush. I fixed my hair three separate times, undoing and redoing it until it was flawless enough I couldn't find anything to fix. Then my dress wasn't falling the way I wanted it to, and the cape was dragging me down. A few last-minute alterations that had Ben groaning did the trick. It was worth it. The cape held much better now and even I couldn't find fault in how the midnight blue dress looked on me.

It needed to be perfect. *I don't want her to ... no,* I thought, *I don't want anyone to see me not looking perfect.*

This wasn't about Gwen. This was about me and my image. At least that was what I was telling myself. I knew realistically I didn't stand much of a chance against her tonight, and, shockingly, I was okay with that. *If she wins the contest, I think I would be okay with that.* I surprised even myself with the admission, but overnight my need to crush her and make her miserable had almost completely evaporated.

I was left feeling some hope for the future. Maybe we could even be friends again. Things would never be how they were before; I didn't think I could let her in like I had before, but maybe we could find a way to work things out, be friends again. I hadn't let myself admit it before, but seeing her made me realize how much I had missed her.

I tried to look around and take in the beauty of the ball, but I caught myself scanning everywhere for that certain redhead. Eli seemed to be looking for her, too, since I kept seeing his gaze darting around the place like mine was.

I didn't know what he had said or done to her, but I knew she would forgive him. She was the type. She was quick to let go of things; we were vastly different in that way. I held onto a grudge. I used to think that was a good thing. I didn't let anyone take advantage of me and stood up for myself. I didn't let anyone walk all over me, but maybe, I was too quick to judge others. I jumped a little too quickly to conclusions. Maybe there might be a little room in my heart for forgiveness after all. At least, for her, I could try.

Chapter Thirty

Gwen

The ballroom was coming alive with laughter as more people filtered in. I tried to focus on Ollie and enjoying myself, but I found myself looking for Lanie. I didn't know if she was still wearing Cassandra's dress, but I hoped so.

Courtney, Skye, and Erin found us and pulled me and Ollie into their circle, talking about the decorations and the songs they wanted to hear. I was grateful they were happy to make us feel welcome. I noticed people were staring at me, and hoped it was for my dress and not the drama from this weekend, although I knew I was going to be giving them plenty to talk about tonight.

When the string quartet played, Ollie pulled me out onto the dance floor and spun me around. I gasped when the walls changed from the ballroom scene projection to bookcases. Ballroom dancing in a library, another dream of mine. Ollie spun me around, making sure my dress flared out before pulling me back to him. I saw Courtney recording and grinned at her, grateful she was capturing this for me. Grateful I would have something to post, but even more grateful I would be able to relive this moment dancing with my best friend in my dream dress at a fantasy ball. It was unreal.

When the music stopped, he pulled me back to the others, but a glimpse of leather armor caught my eye. I turned around and saw Sadie on the arm of a tall Amazonian looking woman. She pulled Sadie out onto the floor and they danced. There was something about it that made me unable to tear my eyes away, unable to stop watching. They complimented each other perfectly, and it was refreshing to see two women dancing, holding each other close without caring what others might think. Maybe that would be me someday.

After tonight, I wouldn't have to hide anymore. I let myself picture Lanie spinning me around the floor, showing me off like that, before shaking my head.

There was a miniscule chance this would work, a miniscule chance she might feel the same, but I couldn't let myself hope. I knew it was likely to be crushed, but there was still hope budding in my heart seeing Sadie and her date dancing. Maybe it wouldn't be Lanie, but someday I could have that, too. Someday I could be openly, unabashedly happy in the arms of a woman I love. Someday.

When the song ended, Sadie's date bowed to her, and Sadie curtseyed. The crowd loved it. I was clapping along with them when I heard Ollie say, "What do you want?"

I turned quickly, hopefully. I wasn't planning to talk to Lanie yet, not until after the contest, but if she was coming to me, then surely that was a good sign, right? But it wasn't her. It was Eli.

I looked back and forth between Ollie and Eli, confused. Ollie looked upset, and Eli looked sheepish. I knew Ollie was protective of me, but his reaction seemed a little over the top. Eli hadn't done anything to hurt me. I was about to say something when Sam swept in and laced their arm around my waist.

"Fancy meeting you here," they said, "although I'm sure you're fancy anywhere."

I giggled, thankful Sam was here to break the tension. I looked at Ollie, but he was still glaring at Eli, who was growing more and more pale by the moment.

"Care for a dance?" Sam asked.

I would have loved to, but there was no way in hell I was leaving Ollie that upset, but Sam leaned into me and asked, "Do you trust me?"

I nodded.

"Then follow my lead."

"But I can't leave Ollie."

"It'll be good for him, I promise. Believe me?"

I gulped, but nodded again.

They pulled me close to them and asked loudly to Ollie, "You don't mind if I borrow your girl for a dance, do you?"

Ollie startled and turned to look at us. Seeing it was Sam, he relaxed a little. He shrugged. "Gwen's choice, obviously."

I gulped. I knew I shouldn't leave him. He was upset about something and I shouldn't leave him, but I trusted Sam.

"Just one dance?" I said, pleading, hoping Ollie would be okay with that and understand. I hated feeling like I was abandoning him, but Sam promised it would be good for him and I trusted Sam.

Ollie looked surprised, but said, "Of course. I'll be over by the bar when you're done."

He stalked off toward the bar, and Sam pulled me toward the dance floor. I looked back and saw Eli was following him.

"What's going on?" I asked the minute Sam turned me back toward the dance floor.

They looked at me with feigned surprise. "With what?"

"I know you have tea and so help me if you don't spill it, I'm not taking another step." I stopped in my tracks and they pouted.

I didn't move.

After a moment, they said, "Fine. You never let me have any fun." I rolled my eyes and let them pull me close. As we started to dance, they said, "Apparently, they have history."

My jaw dropped. That wasn't what I was expecting them to say. "History? What history?"

They wiggled their eyebrows at me. "The romantic kind."

"What? There's no way. They didn't even know each other! Ollie would've said something. Wait, that can't really be what Eli told you. He wouldn't have told you something like that."

"Rude!" Sam exclaimed, spinning me out and then back to them. "You're just jealous I knew before you."

"Definitely not jealous. You're making things up."

"You wish, but since I'm so generous, I'll tell you what I know. Apparently, back before you left, Eli was talking to a guy from out of town."

I thought back and had a vague memory of Eli mentioning him. "The one he was video chatting with?"

Sam grinned. "So you do remember. Well, it turns out that was your Ollie."

"What? There's no way!" I said, even as I was starting to believe him. "Ollie would've told me."

"Eli didn't even tell me until last night. Before, all he told us was that things didn't work out, but he was really torn up about it. Last night, he finally told me that when you left, Mor told him she caught you cheating on Arty with another man and had gone to live with him. When he found out from Ollie that you were coming to live with him, Eli cut things off cold. Apparently, Ollie was supposed to be moving up here."

Now that Sam said that, I did have a vague recollection of Eli mentioning that his boyfriend might have been moving up here, but there was no way it was Ollie, right?

"Are you sure? Please tell me you're messing with me. How did they even meet anyway?"

"Apparently, Eli has family in San Francisco and bought a season pass to be around a certain employee."

"What?! Ollie would've mentioned that for sure. Him and I met there."

Sam shrugged. "I don't know much else or when, just that they met there."

I wracked my brain trying to think of whether I remembered Eli being there that summer, but came up blank.

"You have to be messing with me, right?" I asked pleaded. "If you're not, then I'm the reason they've been miserable."

Their face fell instantly as they looked at me with concern. "I'm so sorry. I got carried away. I should've been more tactful about that. I wasn't thinking, but I can promise you Eli doesn't blame you, and I doubt Ollie does either."

Maybe Sam was right, maybe neither of them did, but it was hard for me to not blame myself. I was the reason they were in this mess in the first place. Well, me and Lanie. Apparently, we didn't just hurt each other. Although that wasn't fair. It wasn't Lanie's fault. If I had told everyone the truth in the first place, this never would have happened. If I hadn't felt the need to hide from who I was, things would be different.

Tonight, I was done hiding. Tonight, things would be different.

Chapter Thirty-One

Sam and I danced a couple more rounds while the wall projections changed. We were dancing in a magical forest and then in the clouds with shooting stars. After a few more minutes, I pulled away from Sam. They knew before I said where I was headed that I was going to find Ollie, but when they said they were going to look for Mor, I hesitated. I hadn't seen Lanie all night, and I wanted to talk to her. I was starting to think it was a terrible idea to confess in front of everyone without talking to her first, but I also knew Ollie needed me.

I was torn, but I ended up turning away from Sam and toward the bar. I was hoping Ollie was still there. I had been a lot longer than I thought I would be, but I wanted to give him and Eli time to work through things. I owed it to them both. I was really hoping they would be able to work things out. I wanted that for him, for both of them.

When I got to the bar, I instantly regretted giving him more time, since Ollie was nowhere to be found and I wasn't sure how I would ever find him with this crowd.

As I stood by the bar, waiting for him, hoping he would come back, I noticed the twinkling, floating chandeliers and lost my train of thought for a moment. They were stunning; right out of a fantasy. I was still watching them when I heard a commotion coming from off to the left and turned around to see what was happening.

The crowd was abuzz about something. I moved closer and saw that Sadie's date was standing in front of her protectively with a dagger in her hand that looked alarmingly real. It wasn't, it couldn't have been, but we weren't allowed fake weapons either.

Sadie was trying hard to pull her date's attention away from the man she was glaring at. He was the tall, dark, and handsome type in a stylish three-piece suit that made him look out of place in a room full of people wearing fantasy clothing.

I was wondering what the fuss was about and why Sadie was yelling at her date. When I saw green flames shoot seemingly out of his hands, I had to do a double take. The flames engulfed Sadie's date. I gasped with the rest of the crowd. Whatever special effects they were using were ridiculous in how realistic they looked.

As we watched, the flames around Sadie's date dispersed, and me and the rest of the crowd looked back and forth between the man, Sadie, and Sadie's date. That had to be the end, right? I looked at Sadie, who looked on in horror at her date. Her date reached out for her with a predatory grin.

I was getting worried. I didn't like the way she was looking at Sadie. Thankfully, Sadie jumped back. Her date swiped out her hand for Sadie again, but a couple of Sadie's friends stepped in between them.

"Inez, come," said the man, calling her like a dog.

I waited with bated breath to see if that was a step too far for whatever scene they were acting out, but she went to him. I knew it had to be a scene they were acting out, but I couldn't have guessed that from how genuine Sadie's fear looked. It chilled me. Sadie took a step forward, but didn't move closer.

Her date had reached the man now. He touched her face, and she leaned into him.

"Let her go!" Sadie shouted with enough force that I figured he would stop. Whatever scene they were acting out had clearly gone too far for her. He would stop and they would all take a bow and we could go back to the ball, right?

He looked at Sadie and grinned. "Hello, love. Just the sorceress I was looking for."

Oh, so she was in on the act, I thought, relieved. I would have to ask her how he got the green flames to work. It would really elevate my cosplays if I could do special effect work like that.

"Why don't you make this easy on everyone and be a doll and come here?"

I shivered at the violence laced in his words. Even knowing it was only an act, he was a convincing villain. I wasn't sure what Sadie was going to do, but I was interested in seeing how this would play out. I glanced around quickly, looking for Ollie to see if he was seeing this, but I still didn't see him.

The man kept talking, "Be rational. You know how powerful I am. I'm sure you'd hate for your friends to see what real power looks like." With that, I and the rest of the crowd collectively gasped when he summoned a ball of green flame in his hand and held it up menacingly.

The special effects were incredible. I could almost believe it was real. A few moments later, the flame went away and he stepped forward. "Fine. The hard way, then. Inez, be a doll and show Sadie what real power looks like."

Sadie's date, Inez, moved forward and in a swift motion, moved the dagger from her side where she was holding it up to her throat, and held it there, pressing it lightly into her own throat.

We all gasped, and I was surprised and impressed to see a thin line of red trickling down her neck. They really thought of everything. They must have set this up with Kodie to do a scene. Maybe it was from Sadie's book since she was involved. If it was, I would definitely read it sooner rather than later.

"If you want your guard dog unharmed, love, you'll come to me," he said.

"Let her go! Stop! You're hurting her!" I looked over and saw that came from Naomi. She was one of Sadie's friends, so it made sense she got roped in, too.

Sadie tried to move forward to him, but another of her friends stopped her. I couldn't hear what she said, but I saw a tear fall down her face. They were really getting into it.

Sadie said something to her that I couldn't hear and her friend looked upset. They exchanged a few more words before Sadie said louder to the girls standing with her, "I'm so sorry. I hope you all have the best lives. You all deserve nothing but the best. Live well and long for me, and try to remember me."

I was surprised by the emotion in her voice and wondered what would happen when she reached him.

"That's right. Come to me, darling."

Even knowing it was an act, I hated the way he was talking to her.

Naomi grabbed her by the arm and yanked her back. "The hell do you think you're doing?" she asked Sadie.

"I don't have much of a choice."

"The hell you don't." Naomi said turning to the man. "Such a big tough boy now that his powers work, huh? If you want Sadie, you'll have to come through us! Or are you too much of a coward that you have to hide behind your powers?"

I wondered if he would 'release' Inez now and 'fight fair'. Based on every book I'd read and movie I'd seen with similar lines, that was what happened when someone challenged the villain's power. It provoked them into fighting fair and losing, every time.

He glared at Naomi. "I have the power here. Unhand her and let her be a good little girl and come to me."

"Just what do you plan to accomplish here?" Naomi asked loudly. "Besides scaring a bunch of women? That's low, even for you."

I was curious, too. I was glad we were about to find out the point of the scene.

"Once Sadie is mine, we'll return to Bancroft and you can go back to your insignificant little powerless lives. Don't you worry."

Bancroft must be a place in Sadie's book. I would have to read it after this. Apparently, she wrote really convincing villains.

Naomi said something to him, but Sadie had my attention. She was scanning the crowd frantically. I followed her gaze and saw a couple of her friends were sneaking up on the man and Inez. I watched them for a moment, wondering if they would go after him or Inez, and was surprised when they angled themselves toward Inez.

It seemed like the more logical thing to do would have been to go after him since he seemed to control her and she had a dagger. I wondered why they decided to do it that way instead.

Maybe for more dramatic effect. I wondered if we were going to get a full-on choreographed fight scene. I hoped so.

Sadie tried to move forward, but Naomi and her other friend wouldn't let her move. I was watching them so intently I was startled to hear, "Okay, everyone, it's time for the cosplay contest!" It was Kodie over the loudspeaker. I gulped.

I had been so wrapped up in the show I had forgotten what time it was. I hadn't remembered to be nervous. It was probably for the better. There was no backing out now. I watched a moment as Kodie moved through the crowd to the man and put her hand on his shoulder, smiling at him.

"I can see we have a couple of contestants here," she said, glancing at him and Inez, "but I'm going to have to ask you to put away the dagger or I'll be forced to escort you out of the building."

The crowd and I all laughed.

I wasn't sure what I had expected, but of course we weren't getting a full fight scene in the middle of the ball. "You all know the rules," Kodie continued. "No weapons tonight."

I was surprised she had agreed to them acting out the scene in the first place with the dagger since it looked so real.

I watched as Inez stiffly removed the dagger from her neck, crouched down, and put it away. Kodie looped her arm through Inez's and led both her and Damien to the front of the room.

"Anyone else who is taking part in the cosplay contest, please make your way up now."

I gulped. It was now or never, and never wasn't an option, but I had hoped to have Ollie with me. I couldn't imagine where he had gone, but I hoped he hurried back.

I was finally going to see Lanie tonight. I couldn't believe she had actually managed to avoid me all night, but there would be no avoiding me now.

I walked forward, and the crowd made room around me. I took a few deep breaths. I could do this. I would do this, and then I saw Lanie.

She was wearing *the* dress. Cassandra's dress from the Solstice ball, the dress that complimented mine. She looked breathtaking. I couldn't take my eyes off her as she moved forward. Her midnight blue silk cape trailed behind her. The dress on her was a work of art. It fit her perfectly; I had never seen her in anything so form fitting and I would have thought she would hate it, but she seemed to be eating up the attention.

Good for her. She was and always had been beautiful to me, but I was happy to see her feeling good about herself.

She was grinning, until her eyes landed on me.

She looked shocked when she saw my dress, taking in the detail on it and understanding what it meant and how it looked like we were here today as Ivy and Cassandra, everyone's favorite enemies-to-lovers pair. I offered her a small smile, a peace offering, but that seemed to shake her out of her stupor. She glared at me, but it was some consolation that the glare seemed halfhearted, or maybe that was wishful thinking.

But no, this couldn't be all in my head. At least I hoped it wasn't, but even if she didn't feel the same, I wanted her to know. Even if she still hated me, I wanted her and the rest of the world to know.

The world! Crap! I was supposed to be filming this. I scanned the crowd again frantically for Ollie and saw him push through the crowd. What shocked me was seeing Eli was in tow and that his hand was in Ollie's. Ollie grinned at me, and I smiled back widely. It didn't matter what else happened. Ollie was happy, so today was a good day.

With his free hand, he held up my phone and nodded.

This was happening, and there was nothing I could do to stop it. No backing out now. I had to be brave. I moved over and tapped Kodie on the shoulder, our signal. She had told me if I didn't that she would move on, giving me an out, but I couldn't take it. If I did, I would never speak my truth, and I was ready.

Kodie smiled at me, and said into the microphone, "I know I said we were starting the cosplay contest, and we will in a couple of minutes, but first Gwen has something she wants to say."

I could feel the microphone shaking in my hand as I took it. I took a deep breath and smiled out at the crowd. "Hi there, everyone. For those of you who don't know me, I'm Gwen, and I hope you'll bear with me as I take a minute to bare my soul to you all. I've been quiet for way too long about this and it's time I finally say something. I'm sick of hiding who I am. For those of you who don't know me, I hope you'll care to get to know the real me after this, but this speech is more for those of you who do know me, and really a particular someone."

I quickly risked a glance at Lanie and saw her cross her arms. My face fell a moment before I took another breath, plastered my smile back on, and plowed on. "For those of you that know me, you know I dated Arty for a long time. He truly was such a sweet man and an even better boyfriend. He was absolutely perfect. I know what you're thinking. If he's so perfect, why'd you let him go?" I paused for a moment. *Here goes nothing.* "I know the rumors say I cheated on him, and those hurt the most. I would have never done anything to hurt him, and I hate that he has to live with strangers calling him clueless and stupid for having been with me. I didn't cheat on him. That's not what I'm here to tell you. There was another reason for our breakup, a reason that Arty has been so chivalrous to keep to himself, from even his best friend, and that's what I'm here to tell you today. He held up his end of the bargain and was more than willing to give me the time I needed, but I'm sick of hiding." I took another deep breath. I could do this. "We broke up because he wasn't my type."

I heard the crowd gasp, and I laughed. "You didn't let me finish. I know, I know, you're thinking, Gwen, how could he possibly not be your type? He's tall, handsome, muscly, and such a patient, kind man. You're not wrong, and if I was at all into men, I'm sure he would have been the one."

Chapter Thirty-Two

Lanie

From somewhere far away sounding, I heard the crowd gasp, but I couldn't take my eyes off her, couldn't process what she was saying, because there was no way. Gwen was straight. She had to be. If she wasn't, she would have told me, right? She had to be straight. This was Gwen we were talking about. I knew her; she wasn't into women. What the hell was she doing? There was no way! Arty would have told me, right? *She* would have told me, right?

"I'm not done," she continued. How could she not be done? How could that not possibly be the only thing she had to say? Gwendolyn Reid isn't straight. That was a big fucking headline on its own. If she wasn't straight, then maybe I was wrong about her. If she wasn't straight, then I was wrong about so many things. How could I blame her for breaking things off with Arty if she wasn't straight? I couldn't. If it were true, I would have been wrong about her and I would be a total ass, so it couldn't be true, right? If she was, I was the world's biggest dick for how I treated her. I gulped.

"You see, for a long time I was okay with being in the closet. I was too scared to tell the world my truth; I didn't feel like I could. I was worried that others would harass me for it, the way they had for me supposedly cheating on Arty."

Fuck. Maybe she was telling the truth. Maybe I was the ass here.

"I worried my friends and family wouldn't understand."

I gulped. She was telling the truth. I couldn't list the amount of times I had felt that exact same way, that same pressure. It wasn't something you could make up. The emotion on her face wasn't something she could fake.

"That the world wouldn't understand."

Shit. I had only been thinking about myself and about Gwen as a person. I hadn't even thought about her platform. I had been out before I ever had a platform. I hadn't had to give coming out to the world and my followers a second thought, because even if they didn't already know, they only needed to take one look at me and they knew, but it wasn't like that for her. She blended in and played the part so convincingly she didn't even set off my gaydar. Not only that, but I berated her for breaking up with Arty and for cheating on him. With Ollie. No wonder she thought it was ludicrous.

"I wasn't ready to be myself, to show the world the parts of myself I kept hidden."

I wondered what changed, what pushed her to be brave enough to come out. A thought struck me that sent a chill down my spine. I hoped it wasn't me. I hoped I didn't accidentally bully her into coming out. Shit, no wonder Arty wouldn't tell me why they broke up. He was with me every step of the way when I came out. He and his family took me in when my mother kicked me out. Of course he would have kept her secret, even from me. God, I *was* a dick. This was all my fault. *The minute she stops talking, I'm going to march my ass over there and apologize, beg her forgiveness. I can't believe I didn't trust her. I can't believe I didn't give her the benefit of the doubt.* This was Gwen we were talking about. I couldn't believe I ever thought she was capable of cheating on and hurting Arty so callously. I couldn't believe I might have bullied her into coming out.

Gwen broke through my thoughts. "Until a woman taught me what it meant to be unapologetically myself." I was hit with confusion. That was the last thing I expected her to say. Did that mean she had a woman? Did that mean this might not have been my fault? "She is fierce, strong, and braver than I ever could be, but I'm trying."

Okay, that couldn't be about me. It wasn't my fault after all, so why wasn't the sick feeling leaving my stomach? It should be good that she found someone, right? That someone was supporting her when I wasn't. *I shouldn't resent that. I should be happy for her, happy that someone was there for her.* So why wasn't I?

"I actually broke things off with Arty when I realized I was falling for her."

My stomach dropped. Who the hell was this mystery woman and what was so great about her that Gwen fell for her so easily? What was so special about her? It wasn't rational, and I didn't understand it, but I already knew I hated her and that she wasn't good enough for Gwen. No one was. Well, Arty was, but he was an exception. No one else could possibly be good enough for her. I defied any woman to try to be good enough for her. It wasn't going to happen.

"Watching her unapologetically, boldly be herself inspired me. Her fire intrigued me, and her soul made me love her."

Leave it to Gwen to be so poetic. So beautiful a declaration, but it was making me want to vomit. I couldn't understand why I hated it so much, though. Maybe it was because Gwen used to be my best friend and I had missed such a big part of her life and the only person I could blame was myself, and I hated that. I hated that she had moved on and found a new best friend. I hated that she had moved on to a new life and found a new love, and I wasn't a part of her life. I hated that the only one I could blame for that was me.

"I realized I would never be happy with just her friendship and that I hadn't had that same fire for Arty. As much as I love and care about Arty, I knew then that he wasn't my person no matter how much I tried to make it work for mine and his sake; he just wasn't her."

What the hell is so special about this woman anyway, and if she's so perfect, where the hell is she tonight?

"And I'm sure you're wondering who she is and why she didn't accompany me tonight. Well, unfortunately, we're still at the enemies stage of our relationship, but I would give the world to change that."

The crowd gasped, and I almost joined in.

What? Who was she enemies with? Who the hell could look at Gwen, could talk to Gwen, and not immediately love her? Who was that immune to her charm?

I looked around the crowd for a moment, as if this mysterious woman would appear out of thin air, but saw everyone's eyes were glued to her. I looked back at her and stopped breathing. She was looking at me. "Lanie, I'm so sorry I hurt you and that I hurt Arty."

I was so confused. I thought she was going to bring up the mystery girl, but here she was issuing an unneeded apology instead. That was so Gwen. I was the one who owed her an apology, but here she was apologizing to me.

I tried to force myself to say something, anything, but couldn't get anything out of my mouth before she kept talking. "It was never my intention, and if you would ever find it in your heart to forgive me, I would be the luckiest girl in the world."

Of course I forgave her. I forgave her the moment she came out to the world. I couldn't stay mad at her. There was nothing to be mad about. If anything, she should be mad at me.

That she wasn't was a testament to how incredible she was. I wanted to say this, any of it, but she kept going. "I wasn't ready to be myself, wasn't ready to admit the truth, until you."

Until me? What did I do?

"Even if you never speak to me again, you changed me for the better and I'll always be grateful to have had you in my life. I don't know that I'll ever have another chance to say this, and this is less than ideal a place for it, but I need you to know... I love you."

My heart stopped beating. I felt the color drain from my face. I couldn't have heard her right, or maybe I did, and she meant she loved me as her best friend and missed me as her best friend. That had to be it, because there was no way in hell she was implying what I thought she was implying.

"I started falling for you long before I realized it myself, and I never stopped."

I stopped breathing. I couldn't think, I couldn't move, I couldn't even blink. I couldn't do anything besides stare at her. She hadn't left any room for doubt. There was no way to misinterpret that. Gwen was in love with me. Gwendolyn freaking Reid was in love. With me. How was that real life? I was the mysterious woman. Shit, *I* was Lancelot.

As that thought hit me, I noticed her staring at me. Shit. I had to say something, but I felt paralyzed. I couldn't think straight. I wasn't even blinking. I had to say something, but her face fell before I could. I opened my mouth, but too late. She had already turned back to the crowd. I closed my mouth.

A moment later, she turned back to me, an unconvincing smile on her face, and said, "I know this is too little too late, but I needed you and the world to know my truth. No more hiding."

Before I could pull her attention back, the host took back the microphone and said, "I am so proud to call you a friend, Gwen, and let me be the first to say I'm proud of you."

Geez, how hard would that have been? To tell her I'm proud of her and that I care about her. I could have said that at least, but instead I was just standing there gaping at her. Maybe I didn't know exactly how I felt, but I knew I cared about her deeply, knew I forgave her, not that she needed my forgiveness. Maybe I didn't know how I felt about her, but maybe we could figure it out together. I watched as the host smiled at her and felt uneasy. Maybe I was lying to myself, maybe I knew exactly how I felt.

"Welcome to the alphabet mafia," someone in the crowd yelled, causing the crowd to laugh.

A couple other things were yelled, but what stuck out to me was a feminine voice yelling, "Do I have a chance, Gwen?"

In that moment, I gained some clarity. I knew enough to know I didn't like that. I didn't like how Gwen's smile turned genuine when she heard that. I didn't like how she seemed to be searching the crowd for the voice. I didn't like the thought of her looking for another woman, the thought of her thinking about another woman.

A few short life-changing moments ago, I hadn't even known she liked women. I had never even thought to consider ever thinking about her like that. I couldn't do that to Arty, right? Thinking about Arty reminded me of our last conversation and the kiss. Arty knew and had given me his blessing. I thought he was joking. I never even considered, but he had *known*. This whole time he had known how she felt about women, how she felt about me, and hadn't told me. If it was anyone else, that would be a grave offense, but this was Arty. I wished he had told me, but as I thought back, I guess he had, in his way. He kept telling me I was being too hard on her, kept begging me to lay off, kept telling me she had her reasons, and I was too stubborn to listen.

The host explained the contest, but it went in one ear and out the other because now I was thinking about that kiss. That *kiss*. That was *real*. She wasn't faking that. I couldn't believe I didn't realize that before. If she really, truly meant that kiss, I was a goner.

Crap. The host was standing in front of me now. I hadn't caught a word of what was happening. She looked at me expectantly before whispering, "Give them your cosplay name."

"Cassandra."

She stared at me longer before seeming to realize that was all I had to say and moving on. I couldn't say anything else. I was too focused on the earth-shattering realization I was having.

Gwen and I had chemistry. There was tension there and *that kiss*. That was a kiss I would beg to experience for the rest of my life. But it wasn't just the chemistry. This was Gwen we were talking about. Gwendolyn Reid, Queen of Cosplay, a goddess among mortals, and she wanted me? I couldn't wrap my head around it, but looking over at her, I knew she wasn't faking her disappointment. She was falling in love with me. She loved me, and I was the worst idiot in the world to think for even a second that I didn't feel the same.

I loved Gwen. *I loved Gwen,* and she loved me, too. Thinking back, the signs had been there. I would have done anything for her. I wanted to spend every second of the day with her. There was nothing too big she could ask of me. I would have done anything for her, and then I messed things up.

I stupidly let her slip through my fingers, but I couldn't let her get away again. I was a fool before, but here and now, I wouldn't make that same mistake. I had to tell her how I felt.

I turned to look at her and heard the crowd gasp. All around us, the walls had changed. I watched in amazement as everyone's character names were listed on the walls. I couldn't believe I had forgotten about the contest. I had been fixated on it for weeks, had so badly wanted to dominate Gwen, prove once and for all that she wasn't better than me, but now it hardly mattered. Now I couldn't care less about the contest, not with her looking so sad steps away from me.

I hoped she won; she deserved it, and then I would sweep her off her feet and tell her how I felt. I would give her a thousand apologies and tell her how wrong I was, how blind I was to not see her when she was right in front of me.

I watched with everyone else, hoping Gwen would win, and was happy to see her percentages shoot up, along with someone named Damien. My own were steadily growing, too, which made me nervous. When mine tapered off, I was relieved. Good cosplay or not, I didn't deserve to win over Gwen. I wanted to see her smile, was desperate for it, and I wanted this win for her.

This was a damn big moment for her, and I was so proud. She had come out to the world. I couldn't get over how brave she was for doing that, and I was relieved that everyone had taken it so well. I knew that wouldn't be the case with everyone online, but I was happy at least that here and now, everyone was being kind to her. I wanted that for her. She deserved that victory. She had taken a big terrifying risk and for that alone, she deserved to win.

When Gwen's numbers tapered off and Damien's kept rising, I was shocked. I hadn't even heard of Damien before. How was it at all possible he was beating Gwen, the Queen of Cosplay? I glanced at Gwen quickly, not wanting to take my eyes off the numbers for long, trying to force the numbers in her favor by sheer force of will, but I was surprised to find

Gwen didn't look sad. I tried to catch her eye, but she was being careful not to look at me.

I had to fix this and quick. I looked back at the wall and saw his numbers still increasing while hers had tapered off. A few moments later, the final tallies came up. Gwen had 26%, but Damien beat her by 16%. I had no idea how it was possible. I registered fleetingly that I had gotten 13% and the rest was scattered between the others, but I didn't care. Gwen had lost, and so had I. A loss to Gwen would have been understandable, expected and ideal, but for her to lose to this Damien we didn't know was insulting. I was just glad she didn't seem upset. I would have fought him here and now for the crown for her if she was frowning.

The host walked over with the crown to him. He was grinning smugly and the douche actually knelt to the ground, waiting for her to crown him. The nerve. I was surprised she indulged him.

When he straightened up, she handed him the microphone. "Bow to me, peasants." The crowd laughed while I rolled my eyes. *Who was this guy? It was ridiculous he couldn't even break character to thank people for voting for him.*

I was surprised to see that one-by-one people actually bowed to him.

I was about to say something when I noticed a green light emanating seemingly from nowhere, seemingly from him. In seconds, it engulfed him, ballooning into a bubble around him. I couldn't comprehend what I was seeing.

He beat his fists against the green haze and I heard him yell, "NOOO!"

The haze around him turned opaque and all that could be seen of him were his fists beating against the bubble engulfing him. A second later, the bubble vanished, and where he had stood, there was nothing.

The crowd applauded and some of the people next to me were talking about how great the special effects were. That was an understatement. It had looked so real it was almost harder to believe it was just special effects.

I only tore my eyes away from the spot he had vanished to look at Gwen, who looked just as mystified by it as I was, not that she would look at me.

After a moment, the host spoke again, "Well, I suppose the rest of the prize can go to our runner-up Gwen."

The host turned to Gwen, but I was surprised to see Gwen shake her head softly. The host leaned the microphone in front of her, and she said, "I really appreciate the votes. Thank you all so much, from the bottom of my heart, but I can't accept this. I feel like it would cheapen what I did tonight. I don't want anyone's pity or to be rewarded for finally doing and saying what I should have long ago. It's important to me you all know I didn't do this to win some contest, so I don't accept, but I do thank you all."

Typical Gwen. She hadn't changed a bit, and hearing that only solidified my need to do what I was planning, what I had to do.

The host moved toward me like I hoped she would, saying, "You're not gonna refuse the prize, too, right?"

She laughed, but when she got a good look at my face, her face fell. Of course I was refusing the prize. As I watched Gwen, I knew what I had to do. I just hoped it wasn't too late.

The host leaned the microphone to me. I smiled and said, "I'm sorry, but there's something more important to me than winning the contest. There's something I have to do, so you can give it to someone else."

It was then that Gwen finally met my eye. As I closed the distance between us, I couldn't help registering the adorable look of surprise on her face. A step later, I reached her and took her into my arms; she melted into them willingly. I dipped her low and leaned down and kissed her, hard. I wanted to kiss that adorable, surprised look off her face, kiss her until neither of us could think straight. Her lips moved against mine with a fervor and passion that surprised me. Her tongue brushed against my lips. I gently bit down on her lip and it was only after her soft moan that I remembered we weren't alone.

When I pulled away slowly, not wanting to part with her, our audience that we had both forgotten about was applauding and cheering for us, but none of that mattered. What mattered was the smile on Gwen's face that lit up the room. Her smile was my universe. I would do anything to make her smile like that again.

That she was smiling like that for me, because of me, was incomprehensible to me. What I had done to get that lucky, I didn't know, but I sure as hell was going to do my best to make sure I stayed this blessed.

I set her back on her feet reluctantly and started grinning like a fool when she quickly took my hand in hers.

She leaned into me, and I almost melted on the spot. She was sunshine, and I was basking in her rays. I wasn't worthy of her, but I would do anything for her and would apologize a million times for how I had treated her. If she let me, I would apologize to her for the rest of our days.

Chapter Thirty-Three

Gwen

I held tightly to Lanie's hand, still not quite believing this was real. I wanted to talk to her about everything. I wanted to get her alone and kiss her again, to whisk her away somewhere private immediately, but people kept coming up to congratulate us. I kept squeezing her hand, needing the reassurance she was here, that she wasn't going anywhere. She squeezed back every time.

After the first wave of people had said their congratulations and dispersed, I saw who I was looking for. Ollie. Still holding Eli's hand. He was rushing over to see us when, all of a sudden, I felt arms around me, tearing me from Lanie. I panicked for a moment until I saw their face and their handsome grin. Sam. I giggled as they spun me around. A moment later, they placed me on my feet and pulled me in tight.

"Missed you," they whispered into my hair.

"Missed you more," I said, tears threatening to spill out.

"Hey! You had your turn. Quit hogging her!"

I quickly let go of Sam, turning around and running into Eli's waiting arms.

"Eli," I breathed out. He wrapped his arms around my waist and I laced my fingers into his dark curls, holding him close. None of this felt real.

"Gwen, we missed you so much."

The tears started falling in earnest then, and when I pulled away, I saw he was wiping away a few of his own. I felt a tap on my shoulder and turned around to see Ben, and was surprised when he pulled me into him, too.

"You're a hugger now?" I said, laughing through my tears. "What else have I missed?"

"Too much," he said in earnest. "You're back for good now, right?"

If I hadn't already been crying I would have started then; as it was, my tears fell faster.

"I'm here for good," I agreed.

"Good," Ollie said from over my shoulder, "cause I'm pretty sure Eli would maim me if I backed out of staying here again."

We all laughed. Seeing him standing hand in hand with Eli, grinning as widely as I was, being surrounded by the people I loved, I felt at peace. The only thing that could have made it better was if Arty were here. I couldn't wait to share the news with him.

I didn't want to move from our friends, but when Lanie pulled me out on the dance floor, I couldn't refuse. I didn't want to refuse.

A couple of hours ago, this was a dream I wouldn't even let myself hope for. I wouldn't let myself picture dancing with her for longer than it took to banish the thought. Now here I was, with her. I hadn't dared to think it was possible. She pulled me to the dance floor, pulling me closer than necessary, but it still felt too far away. I moved closer and felt her chuckle.

It was unreal, and I didn't want to break the spell, but now that we finally had a minute to ourselves, I had to ask her. I pulled back a little, so I could see her face, and asked, "Are you sure?"

She looked confused. "About what?"

"About us. Do you even want to be an us?"

She looked at me, shocked. "Is that even a question?"

It still felt like it was to me. After a moment when my face didn't change, she frowned and pulled me closer, kissing my forehead. "Gwen, I might be an idiot, but I'm getting smarter. I don't know how I was so clueless with you, but now that I know, I'm sure about how I feel."

I took a calming breath before prompting her. "Which is?"

There was a twinkle in her eye when she said, "You have bewitched me, body and soul."

I melted, right then and there. With that line, she took away my doubts. She knew how seriously I took that declaration. I mean, I had only made her watch that specific version of *Pride and Prejudice* with me at least a dozen times. She knew what it meant to me. She remembered. This was Lanie, my Lanie, back in front of me by some miracle.

I grinned, letting her pull me in for a kiss until I pulled away and whispered to her, "Who knew you were so cheesy?"

"What can I say besides I love you? You bring out the best in me and I want everyone to know it. I can't believe I ever thought for a moment that I hated you."

My smile faltered. "I'm so sorry for everything," I said quickly, but she shot me a look that stopped me from saying anything else.

"I'm the only one that needs to apologize. I was incredibly wrong about you and I should have known better. I should have given you the benefit of the doubt. I was just so hurt when you left that I took it out on you. I didn't realize it at the time, but I think even then I was falling for you."

I laughed, batting my eyes at her. "You were a little obsessed with me."

"Understatement of the century."

I started to pull her down for a kiss, but something collided with my left hip, sending me sailing off to the right. Thankfully, Lanie caught me and spun me back to her.

I looked over for the offending object and found Sam grinning at me. They were dancing with a beautiful girl with green hair.

I just laughed and winked at Sam.

I felt fingers graze my shoulder and turned to see Ollie and Eli dancing by, holding each other close.

"Taking good care of my girl, right?" Ollie asked Lanie. Him trying to look stern was enough to send me into a fit of giggles.

Lanie just chuckled and twirled me.

I was surprised to see Ben was dancing, too, and even more surprised when a moment later Sam twirled the girl with the green hair into Ben's waiting arms.

Him being on the dance floor in the first place was surprising since he always said he wasn't much of a dancer, but when I saw the way he was looking at his new partner, I understood.

I leaned closer to Lanie and asked, "Who's Ben dancing with?"

"That's Jade, Eli's cousin."

"Are they...?"

She laughed. "No. She's only been here a few days. They're not anything."

Watching the way that Ben was looking at her, it was hard to believe they weren't anything.

The gears in my mind were already turning for little ways I could help them along.

Lanie saw right through me. "You can't play matchmaker for everyone you know. Sometimes people have to get there on their own."

I sighed. "I know, but my way is more fun."

We both laughed at that and continued to dance. As she held me in her arms, surrounded by our chaotic found family, I knew this was where I was meant to me.

When I met her gaze and stared into her eyes, I didn't want to look away. People were always commenting on my eyes, but I loved hers. There was something intoxicating about them and their depth, like swirls of caramel whiskey that I wanted to stay drunk on forever.

I could get used to this.

Chapter Thirty-Four

Waking up in her arms was surreal. As much as I hoped and wanted her, I never really thought that things would work out. It was like a dream I never wanted to wake up from. That Ollie and Eli were doing the same in the next room was icing on an already perfect morning. I needed to get the tea from him as soon as possible, because them being together was still blowing my mind.

I checked the clock and saw it was getting late, so I reluctantly went to move from the bed, only for Lanie to groan and pull me closer. I let her. I wasn't overly eager to get out of bed, either. We had the Books, Gowns, and Crowns brunch we couldn't be late to, but getting ready could wait a little longer. I knew the second we got there, we would both be under more of a microscope than ever before. Although this time, I hardly minded. I was happy to be seen with her. I didn't mind sharing our happiness with the world. So far, everyone was happy for us, and while I knew it probably wouldn't stay that way, people would have mean things to say, I was happy we hadn't encountered it yet, and I was happy to roll back over into her and lay with her a little longer.

Chapter Thirty-Five

Lanie

Paradise. That was what the morning was. Having her in my arms was a dream come true, one that felt too fragile and perfect to be real. Now that she was mine, now that she was really, truly mine, I would give my all every day to make her happy, to make her feel special. I would spend every day that she let me making up for what an idiot I had been.

We had cuddled and talked for most of the night as we caught up on each other's lives. It was like we never missed a beat, like we picked up right where we left off, just with more touching. I always had a hand on her hip, or her arm, or her back, or was holding her hand. I didn't want to let her go, even for a minute.

When she tried to get up this morning, I didn't want to let her go. I still didn't want to, but I knew we had to get going. I relinquished my hold on her and rolled out of bed, following her.

When we opened the bedroom door, my nose immediately picked up the smell of bacon. I hadn't given any thought to breakfast, but was glad someone had. Probably Ollie or Jade, because Eli never cooked a day in his life.

Gwen reached for my hand, making my heart melt. She didn't want to be any further from me than I wanted to be from her. In less than twenty-four hours, she already had me completely and totally wrapped around her finger and I wouldn't have it any other way.

When we turned the corner, my jaw dropped. There was Eli, surrounded by pans and chaos, pancake batter smeared on his face, bacon sizzling behind him and some of the best-looking pancakes I had ever seen stacked on plates by the stove. My mouth watered as I watched the steam rise from them.

Even with the evidence in front of me, it was still hard to believe what I was seeing. I looked around for another explanation. Ollie or Jade had to be helping him, but no one else was around.

"Morning!" Gwen said brightly, pulling me over to Eli. She let go of me and wrapped her arms around him from behind. He was working on the bacon and didn't turn around. She planted a kiss on his cheek before snagging some pancakes for us and bringing them to the table.

"Since when do you cook, man?"

"Since I have a lot of things to make up for," he said. "Ollie's still in there sleeping. I figured it was the least I could do." He looked at me and added, "Shit, bro, you should probably learn, too."

I laughed and stage whispered, "You're killing me. Don't give her any ideas."

Gwen laughed with us, before saying, "Bacon's the way to Ollie's heart, chocolate's mine."

She didn't have to remind me. That was one of the best things about dating your best friend; I already knew almost everything there was to know about her.

I joined her at the table as we ate, too busy enjoying the shockingly delicious pancakes to say much.

Once Gwen finished hers, she looked toward Eli, who was still cooking. How many pancakes did he think Ollie was going to eat? He had at least ten already done.

"So, are you gonna make me ask?"

Eli kept cooking. "Ask what?"

"What happened between you two last night? How you two managed to keep your relationship a secret from everyone? How you managed to fix things with Ollie?" She rushed out her questions, not stopping to take a breath until she asked them all.

Eli laughed. "Well, it wasn't that hard. I mean, you've seen me."

We laughed, and I heard a door open. I looked over and saw Jade coming out of Arty's room, but she didn't shut the door behind her. Behind her, out came Ben. Jade and Ben? Was there anything else I had missed last night? I knew I was pretty wrapped up in Gwen, but how did I possibly miss Jade and Ben happening? And then, behind Ben, came Sam. Jade, Ben, AND SAM? My eyes were bugging out of my head, and my jaw was on the floor.

Jade saw my face and laughed. "They showed up early this morning, and we didn't want to wake you guys."

Gwen pointed at Jade and the other two, asking what I hadn't been able to form the words to. "So you guys didn't...?"

Ben blushed and Sam laughed, saying, "They wish." Sam ruffled Ben's hair and moved over to Eli's pancake pile, taking some for themself.

"So, what did we miss?" Sam asked.

Gwen grinned. "Nothing. You're just in time. Eli was about to fill us in on the tea."

"That tracks. The bacon and pancakes didn't get your attention, but you'd never be late for teatime."

"Don't I know it," Sam said, laughing. They took over enough pancakes for Jade and Ben, who were already sitting at the table with us, and started passing them out.

"You've probably made enough, you know," Gwen called over to Eli. "Ollie's only one man. Even he can only eat so much." As if on cue, the guest room door opened and out came Ollie. He leaned lazily against the door, looking every bit like he had just woken up, purple bed head and all.

"There's the man of the hour," Gwen said loudly, getting up and running over to him. He moved just in time to catch her when she launched herself at him and wrapped her arms around him.

"Nice to see you, too." He chuckled. He looked around for Eli and looked surprised to find him in the kitchen. "No, really, who made all that?"

Gwen released him and practically pushed him into the kitchen. "Your boyfriend," she said, grinning.

"No. Seriously, who made those? They smell delicious."

Eli grinned. "Glad you think so. Here." He handed him a plate of pancakes with bacon layered on top to form a heart.

Ridiculously adorable. Normally, I would give him a hard time, but I was too blissfully happy, and too happy *for* him, to butt in.

"Don't keep us waiting," Sam grumbled. "Eli was just about to spill the tea."

Ollie raised an eyebrow at Eli. "Oh, he was now? Do tell?"

Eli glared at Sam. They shoved a pancake in their mouth, but started to choke on it through their laughter. Gwen quickly handed them some water that they took gratefully after a moment.

Ollie smiled. "What I think you meant to say was that you were about to tell them our epic love story."

Eli chuckled. "What he said."

"I'm glad I got here in time," Ollie said. "He wouldn't have done it justice."

"To be fair, no one tells a story like you," Gwen added. "No one else would be nearly as dramatic."

"Hey!" Ollie and Sam both exclaimed. Gwen laughed. Ollie looked at Sam, surprised. Sam shrugged. "I'm the dramatic one around here."

We all laughed, before Gwen asked Ollie, "So, what happened?"

"Well, Eli realized how devastatingly handsome I was, how terribly wrong he was, and he fell to his knees, begging me to take him back."

Gwen rolled her eyes. "No, really?"

"I did beg, but I wasn't the one on my knees."

I groaned, throwing a crumpled up napkin at Eli that landed on the counter behind him. "I don't wanna hear that. Get a room."

"We did. Might not want to use the guest room for a while," Eli said.

"Hey!" Gwen added. "That used to be my room!"

Ollie blushed, and Eli grinned. I pulled Gwen tight to me and whispered to her, "You're sharing with me now, baby girl."

She smiled, moving into my lap. "Fine," she said to Eli, "I suppose you guys can have the room."

I pulled her into me, wanting her closer, and lightly kissed her neck.

She whispered to me, "Shhh. I wanna hear this," even while leaning into my kisses.

"And you said we should get a room," Ollie said, laughing. I pulled away from her, waiting for her to move from my lap, but she didn't.

"You don't have to be jealous. I still love you, too," Gwen teased him.

"Just hard to see your ex moving on," he said, laughing.

Eli and I groaned while the others laughed. "You guys are gonna be using that one for a while, huh?" I asked.

"You know it," they both said as I shared a look with Eli. We both had our hands full, and both of us couldn't be happier about it.

Chapter Thirty-Six

Gwen

The second breakfast was over, I pulled Ollie into Lanie's, and I guess now my, room? We had talked last night about me moving in. It should have seemed insanely fast, but it didn't for me. I was already planning to move back to the city, and Lanie and I had lived together for a while. I knew her better than almost anyone else, and moving in with her didn't feel scary.

Ollie and I had the apartment we were looking at that was gorgeous, but it couldn't compare to Arty and Lanie's place. Their place was a cute, good-sized three bedroom with a mostly open floor plan and a balcony. It didn't have the spacious ceilings of the other place, nor the luxurious bathroom, but it felt like home. Given the choice between here and there, I would pick here every time, but it wasn't just me. It was me and Ollie; we were a team.

He was ready to move to the city with me, and I wasn't going to leave him hanging. If he still wanted to move to the apartment, I would. It wasn't far from here and it was a beautiful place. It wasn't a terrible sacrifice to make to have my best friend in the city.

The moment I closed the door, we both started at the same time, "So about the apartment-"

"Maybe you should go first," I said.

"Maybe we should take a seat."

I nodded and nervously sat cross-legged on the floor across from him. He did the same. I stared at him, waiting. A moment later, he blurted out, "I don't think we should sign."

I frowned. "You don't want to move here?"

"Well, actually, that's not what I was saying. Just that I don't think moving *there* is the right decision."

Now I was confused. "Why not? It's gorgeous."

"Come on. You can't really be telling me you still want to live there. I *know* you. I know how much you love it here."

"You *know* me. You know how much I love you. I would live anywhere in the city with you if it meant you were staying."

"Well, I actually had a different idea. Eli and I were talking-"

"Doing more than talking, it sounds like."

He grinned. "What about you?"

I rolled my eyes. "You're not changing the topic. Now, what did you guys get up to last night?"

"What, too shy to share?"

"A lady never kisses and tells."

"It's a good thing you did more than kiss."

I laughed loudly. "Desperate attempt, but no, we actually didn't. Things were really emotional, and we had a lot to talk about and catch up on. We mostly just cuddled, but it was perfect."

He pulled me into him, hugging me. "I'm so happy for you," he said softly into my hair.

"I'm so happy for us," I breathed out, holding tightly on to him.

I didn't want this to change; I hated the thought of him leaving. "You're not leaving me, are you?"

He pulled away, looking serious. "Actually, I was thinking, what are the odds you could convince Mor-Lan- um, what do I call her now?"

"She's Morgana to most, Mor to her friends, so Mor to you."

He looked at me skeptically. "Friends?"

"Yeah, my girlfriend will call you her friend if she knows what's good for her."

We both laughed. "You're a force. She doesn't really know what she signed up for."

I laughed, but he got serious again and said, "I hate giving you away, but I'm glad you're so happy. I'm glad you feel like she deserves you, and she seems to be willing to prove it."

"She doesn't have anything to prove, not to me, but yeah, you know she's going to spoil me. Although I'm not the one that got heart shaped bacon this morning from someone that the entire time I've known him hasn't picked up a pot or pan."

"Honey, you don't wanna know what I did for those pancakes and bacon. By the time I was done with him, he would have done anything I asked."

We laughed, before he seemed to remember his train of thought. "But, anyway, back to Mor, do you think you could convince her and Arty to rent out their guest room for a little while?"

It took me a moment and a couple of slow blinks to realize what he was saying. When I did, I launched myself into his arms and we ended up tangled up on the floor together, but I didn't care. I hugged him tightly and squealed.

"Yes, yes, literally a million times, yes."

The door squeaked open slightly, and I looked over to see Lanie sidling in. "Sorry, didn't want to interrupt. I just needed my-" She stopped mid-sentence when she looked down and saw us. She chuckled and shook her head. I grinned up at her.

"And you wonder why I believed you two were together."

I laughed, and felt Ollie laughing with me.

I looked up at her innocently. "You know what you could do to make it up to me?"

"I'm sure you have an idea or two."

"Ollie's gonna rent the guest room."

Ollie looked nervous, but Lanie rolled her eyes again. "You want your side piece to sleep next door to you? Is that what it'll take to earn your forgiveness? Is that your big favor, Pendragon?"

I almost told her to stop calling me that, but I couldn't deny I liked the way it sounded coming from her. I nodded. "He's worth it."

"Alright. As long as Arty doesn't care, I'm fine with it."

I grinned and told Ollie, "That's a yes. Arty's a sure thing."

"Alright. Well, since you have a room here now, come on and get out of ours."

I couldn't believe she was being so rude until she continued, "We have to be there in ten minutes and neither of you is ready."

Ollie and I exchanged a panicked look before he jumped up and bolted out of the room, closing the door behind him. I turned to her, and she helped me up and pulled me into her. She kissed me deeply, slowly moving us backward until I felt the back of my knees hit the bed and she pushed us down.

I gasped as I hit the bed and her tongue swept into my mouth, dancing with mine for a moment, before I pulled back. "I thought we had to go?" I asked, and gasped when she started kissing my neck.

"We do, but I may have exaggerated how soon."

"How long?"

"A half hour."

"Perfect," I said, before wrapping my legs around her waist and twisting us around until I was on top of her. "Enough time for me to show you how grateful I am."

"You don't have to prove anything."

I gently nibbled on her ear and whispered, "Neither did you. You didn't have to let him move in. I forgave you the moment you asked."

I started laughing and pulled away, but she pulled me back and in a swift move, rolled us over so she was on top of me.

"Such a tease. I'll give you something to laugh about," she said, and started running her fingers up my side, tickling me.

I laughed harder, but before I could beg her to stop, her lips were against mine. I hadn't dreamed that things could feel this perfect, I hadn't dared. I had been hiding in the closet from myself for too long, but now I was out and proud and couldn't wait to continue shouting my love for this woman from the rooftops.

Chapter Thirty-Seven

Lanie

When we all arrived at brunch, we were surprisingly only a few minutes late, although you wouldn't know it from Ben's complaining. That wasn't so out of the ordinary, but Sam agreeing with him was. Sam was always late without fail for everything, and yet today they decided they had to be on time for once in their lives.

I should have known better than to start things with Gwen with everyone around, though. The second we were starting to get hot and heavy, Sam burst in freaking out about how we were all going to be late and we needed to get our asses up and ready.

I could have strangled them, and might have if Gwen hadn't looked so amused by their antics.

Despite Ben and Sam's best efforts, we were still late, but just barely.

There were still people trickling in when we got there, which Eli was quick to point out loudly to Sam. Having Ollie around was already changing things if Eli was complaining about being rushed. From Eli's grumpy attitude, I assumed Sam interrupted him and Ollie, too.

The moment we got inside, Sam rushed off to who knows where. Them disappearing wasn't unusual, but I couldn't help wondering if they might have a someone special. If that might have been the reason we needed to be on time.

Jade trickled off to go sit with some other friends and the rest of us found a table. Gwen picked the table with the rainbow tablecloth. There were probably fifty tables, no two alike, and she picked the rainbow one. I couldn't help but chuckle at how fitting it was for us.

The tables throughout the room were round, and each had eight chairs, except for the rainbow one. It only had seven. With me, Gwen, Ben, Eli, and Ollie, we made five, six with Sam when they returned. We'd have an extra if Jade wanted to float over and visit with us, but I couldn't help but think of who should be in that chair. I missed Arty. I knew he would be home in a week, but I couldn't wait to see him, couldn't wait to tell him all about Gwen and me. Come to think of it, he had been strangely radio silent over the last day. I hadn't said much; just texted a picture of me kissing Gwen on the cheek. I figured that was enough to warrant a video call, but he didn't call.

He hadn't sent back anything at all. If I didn't know better, I would think he wasn't happy for us, but I knew better. I knew better than anyone how selfless he was and how happy he was going to be for us. He had even told me himself to go for it, so I knew I had nothing to worry about on that front, but the silence was weird. I was starting to get a little worried. I'd definitely try calling him right after brunch.

A few of Gwen's friends trickled over to say hi. She grinned when she saw them and reintroduced me. I wasn't thrilled when I realized they were the girls she was sitting with that first night at Kennedy's, but surprisingly, they were all nice to me. I wouldn't have been nice to them if the situation had been reversed, but it seemed like Skye, Courtney, and Erin were nicer people than I was. Their other friend Naomi came over and pulled me and Gwen into a hug. I stiffened, but Gwen's laugh was enough to make me relax.

We heard the host ask us to take our seats and Gwen reluctantly parted with them, making them promise to stay in touch.

After that, we took our seats with the group and I was surprised to see Sam was still missing. A few moments later, the host started their speech. "Thank you all for coming. I truly want to say thank you from the bottom of my heart for making this dream of mine come true and for making this weekend such a big success. If you'll all raise your glasses for a moment, we have a special guest who would like to make a special toast."

I grabbed both champagne glasses and handed Gwen hers. She smiled at me and, for a moment, I was lost in her eyes again. For a moment, it was only the two of us. I was drowning in her. Until I heard the voice.

"Hello everyone."

We both whipped around. It couldn't be, but it was. Arty! He was home early!

'What are you doing here?' I mouthed to him.

He grinned and held up a finger signaling us to wait. I noticed then that Gwen was ready to bound out of her seat, too, so I wrapped my arm around her and pulled her closer to me.

"I'm so sorry I couldn't make it until now and that I missed most of the weekend fun, but I didn't miss the moment that counted. Thank you all for making sure to film and post most of the weekend so I could feel like I was right there with you. If you could all raise your glasses, I would like to make a toast to Kodie, Books, Gowns, and Crown's fearless leader, and to Gwen. To my brave, beautiful Gwen and her proud, loyal Lanie Knight. To finding courage to be yourself and to finding love fit for a fairytale. I love you both so much and flew almost eleven hours straight here because I couldn't wait to congratulate you."

With that, there were tears running down my face and Gwen's. We both raised our glasses to him and he did the same, grinning ear to ear. I took a sip and heard clinking. I groaned, knowing from the one too many romcoms Gwen used to make me watch what that meant, but seeing her smile was more than enough to make me listen to them. I pulled her close and kissed her deeply. The crowd began awwwing at us.

A moment later, we pulled away and Gwen looked at me. "Now?"

"Now." The moment the word left my mouth, we both got up and raced over to Arty. I let her beat me. Arty caught her up in his arms and spun her around like he used to. The moment he set her down, he reached out his arms, and I pulled him in, squishing her into a group hug between us.

"Missed you," I told him.

"Missed you more," he said to me, "and you even more," he said, bopping Gwen's nose.

She laughed, tears still running down her face, but I couldn't have been happier. I hugged them both tight for a moment, before Gwen said, "We should probably get back to the others."

She took both our hands, and like the old days, we both followed where she led.

"I can't believe you came back so quickly. When did you even leave?"

"I might've called him and told him about my plan for the ball," Gwen said over her shoulder.

"You knew he'd come?" I asked her, surprised.

She shook her head. "I had no clue. I just figured no matter how things went, you would need someone to talk to, and I wanted him to be prepared."

By then, we got to the table, and Gwen and I took our seats again. Gwen to my right, next to her, was Ollie, then Eli, Ben, and Sam's open spot, leaving the spot between me and Sam's spot open for Arty.

Arty went around greeting everyone one by one. Sam came out of nowhere and said, "Ha! And you all said I couldn't keep a secret."

"They kept it for about an hour," Ben cut in. "I knew since yesterday."

"Yeah, but you couldn't get the job done," Sam argued.

I looked at Arty for an explanation, who said, "I called the airline the second I got off the phone with Gwen and changed my flight. My next call was to Ben to make sure things went smoothly and to get in touch with Kodie to make sure it was okay I crashed the party. She was enthusiastically for it."

"But Benny boy couldn't get you all out in time, on time, so he called in the big guns," Sam said.

"Really, the big guns thing again?" Eli groaned.

"I needed you all out on time so I could get changed and get here in time to surprise you," Arty said.

"Why didn't I get a call?" Eli asked, sounding offended.

Arty laughed. "I actually tried you, too, but I didn't get through. You must have been busy, which reminds me…" He grinned, extending his hand to Ollie. "It's so nice to finally meet you. I've heard such great things about you, but it's so nice to finally meet and get to properly thank the person who's been taking care of Gwen."

Gwen rolled her eyes. "I'm hardly a delicate flower."

Ollie laughed. "I don't know. I do have to force you to drink water a lot of the time."

She elbowed him, and I laughed hard.

"Seriously, man," Arty kept going, "thank you. I hated the thought of Gwen being on her own, and I'm so glad she had you. I'm so happy to have the honor of meeting someone so important to her and apparently so important to Eli," he said, shooting Eli a 'we have to talk about this' look as he slid into his seat next to me.

"I'll fill you in later," Eli assured him.

Ollie added, "And then, after that, I'll tell you the truth."

We all laughed, before Gwen added to Arty, "Quite the dramatic pair they are. I don't know if I'd trust either version."

Ollie looked at her pointedly. "And public declarations of love aren't dramatic?"

She rolled her eyes and laughed.

"He's got you there, love," I told her.

"Traitor," she replied while still laughing.

"Let's be honest, me and Arty are probably the least dramatic of us all, which is saying something with Arty trying to be Oregon's youngest ever Senator," Ben said.

We all laughed.

As I looked around at our little group, our family, my heart felt more full than it had been in a long time. With Arty here, completing our family, completing our circle, I felt happier than I had in years.

The irony of our queer little family being complete again sitting around a rainbow round table wasn't missed on me.

I raised my glass with a grin, prompting the others to do the same.

"To Arty's return-"

Before I could get further, Arty injected, "To new love."

Gwen quickly added, "To a reunited and expanding Camelot."

Arty and I laughed.

I quickly jumped back in before anyone else could interject. "How about I finish the toast so we can all have a drink?"

Sam laughed. "Speak for yourself." They had two empty glasses in front of them and a third half full in their hand.

"To us, the knights of the rainbow round table."

There were some laughs, but after a moment, everyone repeated, "To us," clinking glasses and taking a drink.

Sitting there with my best friends, with my arm around a girl who was much too good for me, but inexplicably loved me, I was happy.

I didn't know where the future would take us all, but for once, I didn't feel like it mattered. The future would be bright. How could it not be with us all facing it together?

Epilogue

One year later

Gwen

We were running late already, but I couldn't bring myself to care. We'd get there. He knew it and so did we. Time seemed to escape me when I was with her. I guess that was how happiness felt, like time stood still and raced forward all at once. Lanie and her caramel whiskey eyes still took my breath away. I can't believe there was a time I didn't think about her that way, didn't get to hold her, to be in her arms.

"Baby girl," she groaned, sliding her hands around my waist, pulling me close, "we're going to be late. You know Sam's gonna snag the best room if we're not there yet."

I laughed. I couldn't not. She wasn't wrong.

"You won't be laughing when we're stuck next to Ollie and Eli."

I groaned. "Not again." They were ecstatically happy, and I loved that for them. Ollie deserved the best, and so did Eli. I was thrilled they had found each other, but wasn't thrilled to have to hear them going at it through the wall.

Arty had promised this time he was sticking them in the basement so the rest of us could actually have some peace without anyone having to share a wall with them, but if we were late, he would cave.

I knew it, and so did she. Arty was kind to a fault, and was easily swayed about things like that. He had a strong sense of right and wrong, of fighting for justice. He was such a good man, the best really, but his unwavering commitment to doing good, fighting injustice and helping others meant small things like this wouldn't make his radar. He loved me and Lanie, but he loved Eli and now Ollie, too.

"Damn it," I let out, still not pulling away as she held me to her.

"We should hurry," she said, still not moving.

"We should," I agreed, seeing my half-packed suitcase laying on our bed behind me.

This was our big family trip. Our latest, anyway. We were headed back to Arty's family's beach house. The weather had been perfect, and I was excited to see everyone, not that we didn't see them often anyway, but I was excited for the carefree feeling being on vacation would bring, excited for the break from everyday life.

Arty had already left, and Sam, Ben, Ollie, and Eli were probably on their way. We should be going, but I hated packing and Lanie's hands felt so warm on my waist.

Her lips grazed my neck as she whispered to me, "Baby girl, we should go."

"We should," I agreed, "but..."

I turned around and pulled her face to mine, kissing her deeply. The feeling never got old, nor did the little gasp she let out when I surprised her.

A moment later, she pulled away and ducked quickly around the bed. I considered how quick I would have to be to catch her and started laughing.

"We have to go," she said, turning around and getting more clothes for me and shoving them in my suitcase.

I smiled when I saw her put a couple of my favorite shirts, her old shirts, into my bag.

"So impatient," I said, grinning.

"Excited," she corrected. "The sooner you finish packing, the sooner we can hit the beach, the sooner I get to see this on you," she added, holding up my favorite blue bikini.

"Or off of me," I said, smirking.

She put up her hands just as I leapt on the bed, trying to reach her. I landed next to the suitcase, and went to grab her, but she moved out of reach.

I groaned in defeat and moved over to the suitcase, closing and zipping it shut. "There, happy now? All packed with time to spare," I said, glancing at the clock.

"You don't think of time how most people do. If we leave now, we'll be right on time. That doesn't leave anything to spare."

"But if we leave in 20 minutes," I countered, "that will give us some time alone, with an empty apartment and no one to hear you scream."

"As if, Pendragon," she said, using the nickname that she knew still drove me wild. "You'd be the one screaming."

"Why don't you back that up?"

She groaned. "Come on. We'll be stuck next to Ollie and Eli all week if we don't go now. Neither of us will get any sleep."

"It's a good thing I wasn't planning on letting you sleep."

She groaned again. "The things you do to me with those damn ocean eyes. I'm putty in your hands and you know it."

"If that were true, I wouldn't be on the bed alone right now."

"I'm trying to be the responsible one and make sure our vacation gets off to a good start."

"And I'm trying to be a good girlfriend and make sure *you* get off."

She moved toward me, and as I drank in the lust in her eyes, I knew I had won.

As I watched her caramel whiskey eyes dance over my body, I was drunk on her. I needed her *now*.

I couldn't help solidifying my victory. "Besides, I'm betting with what you're planning on doing to me all week, I'll be louder than Ollie and Eli combined."

"Damn it all to hell," she ground out as she pulled me over to her and kissed me into oblivion.

Hers was a high I would chase for the rest of my life, would beg for with everything in me. She was everything, and she was *mine,* but more importantly, I was hers and always would be if I had anything to say about it.

We were late, and we did get the room with the wall bordering Eli and Ollie's, like Lanie had predicted. No one was in the basement, but I couldn't have been happier, so it hardly mattered.

Sitting around the fire pit, listening to the sounds of the ocean with Sam singing campfire songs, I was at peace. Yes, their campfire songs were mostly dirty limericks, but with their voice it hardly mattered. Besides, they were entertaining.

We were celebrating Arty and his first big campaign win. You would think he was conquering the world the way we were celebrating. He wasn't, at least not yet, but his future was looking brighter and brighter by the day. His eyes were full of hope and his vision, full of stars. He saw things and people not for what they were, but for what they could be. He was determined to make the world a better place, and I knew better than to doubt him when he put his mind to something, so here we all were celebrating the present, but also what was to come. It was going to be a hard road, but if anyone could walk it, it was him.

Looking around the fire, I saw Arty was talking animatedly to Ben with Eli and Ollie cuddled up together, listening. One of Ollie's hands was in mine, and I was cuddled up against Lanie. I burst out laughing at the look on Lanie's face when Sam found new inspiration and started back up. My heart felt full; I felt at home.

I was proud to call every one of these people my family. I loved them all with everything in me and couldn't help but think how lucky I was that the universe, fate, whatever you call it, had smiled on me and brought them all into my life.

I grinned at them all and raised my cup, saying, "A toast, to Arty being well on his way to being a big fancy politician and changing the world."

He blushed and countered, "To us, our family, and the great things we have done and are yet to do."

I couldn't have said it better myself.

"To us," we all echoed.

I couldn't wait to see the great things we were yet to do, because one thing was for sure, our future would be bright.

THE END

So, what did you think of Cosplay and Confrontation?

I would love to hear any and all of your thoughts! If you would be so kind as to leave any review it would be greatly appreciated. Any review, good or bad, short or long, is always welcome.

Check out *Off Script*, which tells the story of Sadie, a fantasy author whose first convention goes haywire when her characters literally jump off the page.
Gwen and Lanie's story was born from Sadie's and plays out in the background.

For updates on my next book or to tell me what you thought about this one, you can find me:
Visit my website: Thelibraryofsarahzane.com
Or follow me on TikTok or Instagram: Libraryofsarahzane
Like my Facebook page: Sarah Zane (libraryofsarahzane)

My TikTok is hilarious if I do say so myself.

Please come find me on any of those platforms, I would love to hear what you thought about my book!

ABOUT THE AUTHOR

Sarah is an author of happy endings for traumatized queers.

She is a bisexual feminist and a licensed therapist. Her stories deal with themes of feminism, trauma, sexuality, and mental health.

She lives in New England with her husband and 2 black cats named Gatsby and Mr. Darcy. When she isn't writing, she can be found perusing a book in her home library, making chaotic book themed videos for TikTok (aka Booktok), taking forest walks, visiting castles, planning exotic trips she can't afford, or cuddled up with one of her cats crying over fictional characters yelling at them about how badly they need therapy.

For more from Sarah Zane, check out…

Beautiful Little Fool.
A sapphic, feminist retelling of the Great Gatsby from Daisy's POV.

Forbidden Love, A reputation in ruins.
How much will she risk for a happy ending?

Sequel coming soon...

Of Masks and Magic

A fantasy and fantasy romance charity anthology which features two full length novellas from Sarah Zane

Under Lock and Key is a sapphic cozy fantasy romance story with a dark twist. The story follows a lonely innkeeper and her mysterious guest.

The Lost Princess is a fantasy adventure story with court intrigue and a dash of romance. The story follows the lost princess's return to her kingdom and the masquerade thrown in her honor.

Of Masks and Magic is only available for a limited time, and the stories may or may not be republished in the future.

ACKNOWLEDGEMENTS

First and foremost, I want to thank the girl with the ocean eyes for telling me my own boring brown eyes look like swirls of caramel whiskey. It was a compliment I won't ever forget. To that girl who inspired this story but is still looking for her own happy ending, I'm so proud of you for everything you've been through and how strong you are. I am in awe of you. I hope you never lose your sense of hope and can't wait to see what the future holds for you.

To Emma, who wrote a Pride and Prejudice retelling that I'm obsessed with (*Pride Pancakes and Paris* by Emmie J Holland, go look it up, you'll thank me later), thank you for making me jealous enough of your brilliance to push me into doing my own spin on Pride and Prejudice. I can't wait to read more of your stories. Also, thanks for being my friend. I adore you.

To Jordan, who wrote *A Ripple of Power and Promise*, thank you for bringing such wonderful dynamic characters to life, and thank you for agreeing to let me borrow them for the sake of my story. I adore you and am so ridiculously proud of you. (And yes readers, *A Ripple of Power and Promise* by Jordan A. Day is a real story and you should definitely go check it out).

To Jess, thank you for letting me force you to be my author mentor. Thank you for being there for me through all the ups and downs of authordom and thank you for being you. I'm so happy to call you my friend.

To Connor and Priscilla, thank you both for being my queer crew, my follow rainbow road residents, my right hand gays. I adore you both. Thanks for listening to me bitch about plot holes and rogue characters.

To Books, Gowns, and Crowns (aka Jordan and Kodie), thank you both again for existing and for creating such a wonderful space for readers to come together and live out their fantasy dreams. I can't wait to see you both again for Chapter Three.

To Josh and Alex, thank you both for having dynamic enough personalities that they unconsciously seep into my characters. (Here's hoping you never actually read this, but if you do, know that I love you both.)

To My Leos, thank you for being there for me through everything and for continuing to be there for me. I adore you both more than I can express.

To my Books, Gowns, and Crowns family, I love you all and hope to see you all again soon. Thank you all for the support and for being such wonderful people.

To Cas, you know why *wink wink*

To my husband, thank you for continuing to support me in my dreams and encouraging me to keep going.

To my mom, thank you for embarrassing me by telling everyone you know to read my books. The support means the world to me and I'm incredibly grateful that you love and support me and my books.

To the rest of my family and friends, thank you all so much for the love and support. It means more to me than I can express. There are way too many of you to list here, but know I appreciate you.

Thank you to my beloved Booktok community of wonderful authors, readers, and new friends. I have so much love for you all and am incredibly happy to have found such a great community that makes me feel so at home.

Last but not least, thank you to you, dear reader, for reading this and helping support my crazy dream of being an author.

From the bottom of my heart, I love you all.

Printed in the USA
CPSIA information can be obtained
at www.ICGtesting.com
BVHW041457180823
668707BV00002B/7